i AM Anna

a novel by

ANN LEON WHITE

SUN SWEPT PRESS

Library of Congress
Cataloging-in-Publication Data Available on Request.

ISBN 0-9768804-2-3

Sunswept Press
P.O. Box 1664
Los Angeles, California 91614
www.sunsweptpress.com

First Edition

Printed in the United States of America by
Malloy Incorporated, Ann Arbor, Michigan

Cover Design: Dalton Design
Cover: Details of photographs by August Saltzmann, 1854

Interior Design and Production: Robert S. Tinnon Design

Publisher's Note: Though at times historically inaccurate,
certain discrepant terms, names, and places have been included
in the context of the novel inasmuch as they remain
true to the imaginary tenor
of Anna's voice.

To Caesar Pacifici and Henry Gatton,

and above all to my family,

with gratitude

CHAPTER I

ANNA

I am Anna, wife of Ezekiel, mother of Mary, and grandmother of Jeschu. Jeschu was born to be the Messiah known as Jesus. I cannot find peace until I tell the true story of our family: my husband, Ezekiel; my daughter, Mary; and her husband, Joseph. My story is of the love and travail we experienced following the birth of Jeschu. These memories have haunted me through time. I want to free myself from them and show you what love intertwined with destiny can bring.

I am not going to tell you this story as if I knew what happened but as if I did not understand anything, as I am not able to fully recall that life myself. Still, there are memories of it that haunt me. If the story has meaning for you, then it is good. If it does not, then you will not be sorry anyway as you will have learned what we experienced following the birth of Jeschu.

My story begins with my childhood and the revolt against the rigid beliefs and practices of the holy white-robed Essene Hebrews in Palestine, who were devout in their worship of

God but denied women the right to be more than servants, obedient slaves to their husbands, and worst of all, forbade them to read or express an opinion.

The memory starts with my strong-willed rebellion against the precepts of my father and continues with the effect of the cry of my grandson's soul from a cross left on us all. He used his right as a rabbi to express his beliefs, and his rebellion rose against the interpretations of the Mosaic laws of the Hebrews.

"You are possessed by evil spirits," my father, a rabbi, used to say to me, flinging those words at me when I refused to obey his orders. Such disobedience as mine was unheard of among women.

My defiance, I believe, was preordained. For a powerful flow of strength came through me when I spoke my pain at my father's insistence on absolute obedience. Such a power, I believe, also sustained my grandson, Jeschu, throughout his trial when the priests of the Sanhedrin accused him of blasphemy.

Mary, my daughter, knew no fear of any authority. Her faith and strength far exceeded my own. Mary claimed she spoke with angels, but I didn't believe in them. I saw Jeschu suffering cruel treatment from the Romans and his own people. He was seen everywhere, in the hills and in synagogues, a tall, blue-eyed Semite, bone thin, a white gown and robe wrapped around him, his feet in worn rope sandals caked with the sand and rocks he walked on. Crowds gathered whenever he and his disciples stopped to rest or eat or talk. Always people came with their sick ones, begging him to perform some kind of miracle. He stood hour after hour scourging demons and healing the sick. Often, when I stared into his face, I would be blinded by the light darting from his eyes like flashes of lightning.

"Grandmother," he would tell me, smiling as he cupped my chin in his hands, "always let love shine through your eyes. Keep love alive there and you can heal the world."

But I could not put love in my eyes. The threat of death hung over my grandson's head, and it caused me to look at the world with alarm. Many times I put ointment on the cuts and bruises he endured from rocks thrown by young boys.

I am getting ahead of my own story. I begin with my life as the daughter of a strong, self-willed father, Joachim, and Deborah, my mother, his wife and slave.

I was a child with strong feelings of love but not of obedience to Papa, a holy man, a rabbi. I particularly remember a time when I was fourteen, lying on the earth breathing in its fragrance, the profuse and pleasant flowers of spring. Papa came upon me as quietly as a stalking hunter, then pounced, putting his face so close to mine that I could see the hairs in his nose and the rage in his eyes.

"What are you doing, lazy girl?" he barked at me. "Go and help your mother!" Then he waited for me to stand up and take myself back to our dark and gloomy cell, where my mother was always working, doing something. He roared at me, "Anna, give up your rebellion. God made you a woman. A woman is a person meant to serve man in whatever way he needs. This means that you are to have deep feelings for your father or your man, not yourself."

His words did no good. I would not help my mother when he was around in spite of my fear of him.

We lived in an Essene cloister of dark caves. The Essenes were an ascetic Hebrew sect with cloisters the length of Palestine. Our cloister was in Bethlehem in Galilee, not in the village of Bethlehem you know to be in southern Judaea.

I knew secret recesses in our caves and often hid myself for an entire day when Papa was home. Or I climbed strong oak trees along the river that emerged from beneath the caves and hid for hours in their branches, lonely and afraid. There were no other children in the cloister, and I sometimes spent my time crying and dreaming of the day I would be grown; a day when I could find my own husband, a man who would be kind and thoughtful and treat me with love and tenderness. We would have children and animals and laugh and love all day long. We would not be bound by ritual and prayer, but by our love.

Every day that he was home Papa would say to me, "Anna, change your ways or I am going to have you beaten for disobeying me. When you are a woman, before you are given in marriage, I will have you whipped to cleanse you of your evil spirits."

"I do not have evil spirits, Father. You give me orders as you would a slave." I had only a vague idea what I was talking about. I had never seen or heard of a slave except in witnessing a conversation Papa had with a man about the Romans who ruled our country.

"Slaves are better treated than we are," the man had said.

"Who are slaves?" I asked my father.

"They're people like you who do not obey orders. Then there is a fight and if they lose, the winning army takes them to their country to do all their hard work. If they don't obey, they are killed. That is what Romans do if you fight them when they want to take your country away.

"Essenes do not have slaves," he continued, "but I can have you whipped for the evil spirits in you because they defy me. Ten holy men will gather to hear the evidence against you and then witness the beating you will be sentenced to. No woman has ever been given a beating. You will be the first. You will be branded and excommunicated for the rest of your life as the only woman in our cloister ever to disobey her master. Is that what you want?"

"No, I do not want that, Papa, but I will not obey you like a slave."

I wanted to fight back against the terrible injustice of men in the way they treated their wives and daughters, even if I got a beating.

I fought Papa in small ways, which was annoying to him. I hid his scarf and the little coverings he used for his fingers and all his paper writing equipment. I took away many of his prayer items: a mezuzah, the sacred words in the doorpost, and a little reading of the Torah in his room. I hid them in the broken limb of an old oak tree. Then I went to his room when Mama wasn't around and took some of his clothes and hid those so he could not find his robe or his slippers. I hid everything. Papa raged at me and threatened to throw me out of our cave dwelling. When I left, winding through some dark passageways to an unused entrance to the cloister, I would climb a tree or two and then go to my hiding place and take out his clothes, sometimes rained on and always wrinkled. Papa slapped me hard for this.

"Wait and see," he said. "One day, you'll wish you had behaved better."

Papa said again and again that I was born with evil spirits. "You are dark; your eyes are black. You have no light in you. You are an ugly girl. You will become a curse to whoever finds you and takes you. I pity him." He would spit at me then, and I would run from the room. Mama never said anything to Papa to defend me. But she often bemoaned her lot to me, that she had a daughter with so little appreciation of her father. I should understand him and obey him, and then life would be much better for me and for her.

Papa moved like a fox in stealthy ways when he came into the house. His thin body was always clothed in white robes. He had glowing, liquid brown eyes from all his praying, a large straight nose, and curly black hair. Papa never cut his beard, which was also curly and black and reached almost to his waist. His face was not handsome, but I admired his looks.

Mama's face, when she was young, was more beautiful than any I had ever seen. "You are as beautiful as an angel," I once told her. I loved to look at her oval brown eyes, which were set in a perfect oval face that was creamy in color. Her pain at the cruelty of my father, who did not treat her at all like a woman of beauty and sweetness, could be seen in how she carried her slender body: bent over, silent, like a dead person who just walked around, trying to stay awake.

Papa never showed Mama any affection or gave her any kind of praise. She was his possession, and he was her master. There was no doubt about that. Papa did not consider me a possession. He asked nothing of me because he knew I would run away and hide if he did.

Essenes do not usually beat women, but Papa insisted that I was intractable and filled with evil spirits. As he told me many times, before I was given in betrothal, he wanted me to have a strong whipping in order to remove the evil in me and show me what God expected of me as an obedient woman.

One day he came to me and said, "This is the day you are to get the whipping I promised you."

Mama ran to him and tried to grab his arms. "You cannot do this, Joachim. No. She is your daughter. You will bring disgrace on us for all our lives. Do not do this."

Papa pushed her away. "It is time for us to remove the evil spirits in her," he answered, red from rage. "Come with me. You will have a good beating, and then the spirits will leave. Then you will be my daughter."

I could not get past Papa to run away. My eyes darted to my mother. She stood still and quiet, her face drawn and white. Her eyes told me she could not answer him or forbid him. She would not stop Papa. He grabbed me by the arm. I tried to pull away from him, terrified of his powerful body and his will, his heavy breathing. "Now you will get it. Now you will learn what it means to defy your father, a holy man."

"How can you do this to your daughter?" I asked him. "Please, let go of my arm. I won't run away."

He released me and pulled me past our living quarters, past the warmth and candlelight and my mother's tears, down dark corridors and down again into caves I did not know existed. We came to a cell buried on the lowest level, lighted with a row of candles. Ten acolytes, or rabbis, dressed in their white robes, waited there in a row, their heads bowed as they prayed to Jehovah. I did not know what they were praying for. I looked for recognition, a face to acknowledge me, but not one of them looked up.

"This is the woman? This child? She defies you?" Rabbi Ebenezer asked my father. At this point some of the young rabbis looked up, cupped their chins in their hands, shook their heads as if puzzled, and went back to their prayers. All of them had long beards, black hair, very pale faces with enormous brown eyes under heavy black brows, and high, chiseled cheekbones.

"This girl is evil," Papa said, pulling at his beard. "Since she was young, she has disobeyed me. She will not give me any attention, serve me food, or clean my clothes. My wife must do everything and this one will not help. She took my holy robe and hid it. Another time she hid my robe and my slippers. I lost my temper and slapped her hard. Then she took my things again, and I slapped her again. Since she was a small child, Anna has questioned my authority over her. She has not learned her place and she has not learned to serve man, her master."

The rabbis didn't answer him but talked among themselves as I stood in front of them in the white linen robe worn by women of the Essene faith, trying to hide my fear, humiliation, and shameful feeling of being despised. In spite of my desire not to cry, tears spilled out. I managed to say, "This is not right. You don't own a human being, and we are human beings, not animals."

Father slapped me hard, and I saw he was ready to punish me at last for all the years he'd waited to do it. Papa looked up at the other rabbis for their permission to continue with the whipping. They nodded to him. My father tied my wrists with a leather thong and pushed me against the wall facing him. His anger terrified me.

"Papa, don't. Please, don't," I begged him. I thought he wanted to kill me, but the master rabbi, Ebenezer, motioned him to stop.

"She deserves a whipping," Papa insisted.

Rabbi Ebenezer spoke. "We can whip her if you feel she has evil spirits in her. But as her father, you cannot apply the whip." He turned to a rabbi next to him. "Call Jacob and tell him I have need of him."

When Jacob showed up, he looked like the other rabbis in his white robe, bare feet, and black beard. He must have been standing outside the door waiting for a signal, because he was in the cell before he was called. Rabbi Ebenezer handed him the bloodstained stripping whip of leather thongs that lay on the floor. The stink of it filled my nose and that, combined with the sting of the slap my father had given me, caused me nearly to faint. But I would not. I will not faint, I promised myself. I can stand this.

Jacob said, "Is this the person you want me to whip?"

There was a pause. None of the rabbis spoke. "I will never hit a woman or beat a man with this thing." He started to fling the whip onto the floor, but Papa shouted, "Then I will!" He forced the whip from Jacob and, with all his strength and rage, hit me across my face and breasts. The other rabbis grabbed Papa and stopped him.

"You will do penance for this, Joachim," Rabbi Ebenezer said. I fell to the floor in great pain, my face bleeding.

Rabbi Ebenezer shook his head again and again, puzzling over what to do about me. "Joachim, she is a young girl, very stubborn, but I do not feel evil in her. She has defied you. She should be punished for that. You are entitled to respect and obedience from your daughter."

I do not know how long the rabbis spoke among themselves. Finally Rabbi Ebenezer came to me where I lay on the dirt floor. He stared at me for a long time. I could not say anything. My face and body were swelling, and blood was dripping onto my robe. Finally, the rabbi spoke.

"You are excommunicated for your disobedience. You may remain in the cloister with your mother. No one here will be permitted to speak to you except your mother. You may not attend prayers. We would tell you to leave, but you are too young. Perhaps you will change."

But I knew I would never change, because I had a destiny. I was sure of it. I would not live as a slave.

"Oh, Anna, Anna, my only blessed child," my mother often said. "You must accept our fate. You must realize we cannot fight men who provide us with food and shelter and give us our children. Don't you want a husband and children? Don't you want to live with us here?"

I heard those words over and over, and I did not answer. If I had, I would have shown the rage I felt, like a desperate, trapped wildcat who snarls and snarls, threatening but helpless. I didn't understand how Mama could accept the kind of treatment that Papa gave her year after year. The one pleasure in her life came from giving birth to me, her only child.

After the whipping, Papa packed his robes and scrolls. "I'm going to Qumran," he told my mother. "I cannot live here with an unrepentant daughter. Evil spirits are still in her."

Though I was to be ostracized as a person with evil in her soul, I was free to go as I pleased. Never will I live as they do, I vowed. I will never be subservient. A woman has a brain and a body. Why must she be classified as either whore or slave? Papa in his ravings had often called me a whore, even when I was a child, because I did not show him the deference he expected.

I did not know what love was, but I thought there must be somewhere a man who would share his life with me without making me a slave. There must be, I said aloud many times.

Beauty gave me joy, and God had spread beauty everywhere—on the land, in the earth, and in the stars and sky. But where was our people's joy in life? Why did the Essenes believe that suffering was part of worshiping God? Why weren't they free and open with each other? Why didn't they give each other help and information instead of pretense and lies? No one spoke their feelings, not my mother, not my father, not the few people I knew in the cloister.

Papa read from the Torah and gave lectures on the purity of life as a worshiper of Jehovah. All of the rabbis sat on a bench and sang the words they read in a rhythm, bending back and forth with their heads. They had many laws of purification, and if a rabbi was guilty of making a wrong absolution or walking in the wrong space, he was given very strong punishment. God is Jehovah and he protects us. I wondered what he protected us from since we had so little pleasure in our lives. The main desire, it seemed to me, was to be miserable and in that way please Jehovah.

And yet I felt love and passion brimming up in me when Papa read from the Torah. The glorious words of love and praise to God brought me into a bliss of joy and love. I wanted to live in that bliss and share my life with someone who felt the same way.

"My God, Jehovah, I am praying to you. Help me. Do not let me die, starved and beaten. Because if I leave here with no protector, I will suffer from the hands of any man who finds me. Oh, God. I want to be wise and understanding, loving and good. I do not see that all the studies these men are doing change them. They are cruel. They will not stand for me. I must leave."

I did not know what to do. I did not want to run away like an animal banished from its family, which would surely guarantee a destiny of starvation. I did not dare to do it. Bethlehem was a tiny village with one dusty, rocky road lined by stalls, then a block or two of houses hidden in masses of trees. Most of our people took care of their own needs, growing their own fruit and vegetables, tending their lambs and sheep, their chickens and geese and ducks. There was little need to buy anything other than oil, woven cloth and hangings, jewels and pottery, or robes for wearing. This is what the shops sold. Inside our houses, a single garment of rough cloth covered our bodies.

I could not leave the safety of the cloister until I found a new place to live. I spent long hours away from home visiting with my friend Rebecca in Bethlehem.

Rabbi Ebenezer came to Mama one afternoon after one of my visits with Rebecca and, while I was mending a pretty red cloth for our table, told her that since I had not found someone to marry, he had followed the custom of the cloister and had betrothed me to Malach, an Essene rabbi like Papa. Malach would give me the same life Papa gave my mother.

"No!" I spoke in a strong way. "I'm twenty-two, too old for marriage. Please free me to live without it." I begged the rabbi to tell Papa that I refused to honor this betrothal.

Malach, a thin young man with his long beard and hair nicely washed, came later to talk to me. He had seen me many times but had never spoken to me. I had nothing to say to him. He had nothing to say to me. My face showed my unhappiness. My betrothed remained silent for a few minutes while he looked into my eyes.

"Would you like to be free of this betrothal?" he asked.

"Yes, I would."

"It is a matter of indifference to me. You are released," he answered, a faraway look in his eye.

I blessed him for the remainder of his life and forever as a tightness lifted from my heart. I wanted a husband who cared for me and would love me as a man can love a woman. He would want me to love him back. Neither of us would be bound by ritual or prayer, only by our love for each other. I knew nothing of sexual love. My idea of love had come from stories, the story of Abraham and Sarah, of Isaac and of Jacob. Jacob, who worked for seven years to earn his love, Rachel, but was given her sister, Leah. Driven by love, he worked another seven years and eventually married Rachel, his true love. I wanted a man to love me that way. If I couldn't have that, I wanted no one.

One sunny summer day, dusty and hot, Rebecca and I walked to the village to find some thread her mother wanted. It was there I saw Ezekiel for the first time. When he came into my sight, I knew he was my destiny.

A thousand lights filled the air. A current of electricity shot between us. My head buzzed. He turned to stare at me. His eyes pierced through me and left me buzzing. He smiled. I lowered my head and saw that his hands had firm, brown fingers hardened by work, not the pale white fingers of a rabbi. His dark curly hair hung in thick ringlets around his neck and over his ears, framing his face. A beard, black as a storm cloud, covered his chin. This man was as lean as my father but taller. After that first glimpse, his image was emblazoned into my brain. Neither of us spoke.

I saw Ezekiel again the following week. Rebecca and I had gone to the village to draw water at the well. He was waiting there in the hot sun as if he expected us. He walked toward me, a smile on his face. A warmth hotter than the sun enveloped me. I panicked, dropped the bucket I had filled with water, and watched it drain away, keeping my head down and not looking at him. Ezekiel laughed.

"You are the real and beautiful girl of my dreams," he said in Aramaic.

I didn't answer.

"What is your name? Do you live in this village?"

It was forbidden for me to talk to a man, especially a stranger. I ran rapidly away from the well, leaving Rebecca to refill the bucket. "Who was this man?" I asked Rebecca when she got back to her house.

"He's a stranger, but I know who he is," Rebecca said, giggling, as she remembered how I had run away. "His name is Ezekiel. His father lives in a cloister in Qumram. Isn't he handsome? Ezekiel, . . ." she paused, teasing me with her smile. "Ezekiel likes you a lot. I saw that. He asked about you after you left, but I told him nothing. Then I spoke to our neighbor, Hannah. He is staying at her house. She told me he is a strong man, very kind."

"Is he an Essene?" I asked. I prayed that he was because, despite how Essene men treated their women and how my father treated me, I could not see him again if he was not. There is an important law about the blood of the Essenes being purified for the coming of the Messiah. Essenes must marry Essenes.

Rebecca answered, still smiling her laughing smile. "Ezekiel is Essene. His mother is from Judaea, and he is not betrothed."

I went through my chores for Mama pretending I was Rachel at the well, beautiful, but loved by Ezekiel, not Jacob. I came alive with joy and found myself singing. Chores were nothing. I knew Ezekiel and I would be married. Destiny had made this match. I thanked God with tears.

"You look different," Mama said when she saw me that evening. "You look so happy. What happened? Did Malach change his ways and now he pleases you?"

I gave her a kiss and said, "I found the man I want to marry, Mama. You will love him. He is so different. He is so kind. I can tell even though we have not spoken. I know we are to be married."

"What are you saying? You are betrothed. Why do you say you have just met your husband?" Mama's hands stirred a pot of thick soup that sent up a strong aroma of spices and vegetables, which we were to have for dinner with bread and cheese and some of our delicate figs. She didn't stop stirring. "Papa picked out Malach. He is a good man and a great scholar. Papa is fond of him."

"I spoke to Malach today, Mama. He said he would release me because he didn't have any feelings one way or another about marrying me. Even if I do not marry the man I saw by the well, I will not belong to Malach, who is a very cold man. He will never give me any kind of happiness."

Mama did not agree. "You must marry Malach," she said to me. "If you do not marry Malach, what will become of you? Papa will throw you out of our place. You will have nowhere to go." I smiled and thought to myself: *I am going to marry this man I have never spoken to, and we will love each other for our lifetimes.* Mama shook her head and sighed at the way I acted. She was used to it.

"You have not met this man. Why are you so certain he feels as you do? And what do you know about him? You know you must marry an Essene, and you must not defy Papa. You will need his permission."

She tasted the soup and nodded her approval of it. I looked at her hands. This beautiful woman, my mother, had the reddened hands of a toil-worn old person, her fingernails browned and broken from smashes of the hammer when she tried to nail a board. Her shriveled fingers spoke of years of heavy labor. I wanted to cry for her.

"Try to be more understanding of Papa," she added. "He has a great problem in his own work. He does not want to be a holy man, but he cannot break his vows. He would like to be a teacher of men but not a holy man."

"Why do you not move away from the Essenes?" I asked. "They are a very cruel group of people who make you do things you don't want to do and make you deny your flesh and your soul. It is always God."

Mama smiled. "Papa will never leave the Essenes. They gave him great truths, and he is ready to die for them."

Ezekiel and I never talked, but our eyes did when we saw each other in the village. Then he stopped me one day to tell me he wanted to marry me.

"I asked your father at Qumran if he would bless our union. I told him, 'I deeply want to marry your beautiful daughter, Anna, and I swear that she will not lack for anything if you give me permission to marry her.'" Ezekiel smiled, remembering Papa's response. "He just laughed at me."

Ezekiel's father, it happened, lived in the same cloister at Qumran as Papa. They shared hours of time together, so Papa gave his consent.

"You do not belong here," Papa said to me when he came back. "This man you want to be betrothed to is born an Essene, but he does not practice the faith the same way his father does. I will give my consent to this bonding, but you will no longer be considered an Essene. You will no longer come to the cloister, and we will not visit you."

I hardly listened to what he said. Of course we would be with them. Papa was testing me, I thought. But it turned out he was not. The cloister of the Essenes closed its door to me forever, just as my father said would happen.

Released from the shackles of my father, I found myself running and skipping like a child, full of energy, bursting with the joy of deliverance.

I stayed with Rebecca until the betrothal could be arranged.

"You are a very fortunate girl," she said. "This man is in love with you. And he's an Essene. His father and yours are friends. It is hard to believe. I have never met a man I wanted to love."

"You will, Rebecca," I promised her. "Just wait and see. Someone will come for you."

Ezekiel made the plans and prepared for the betrothal ceremony with the village rabbi.

My parents did not come to the ceremony. They were pleased I had found someone to love, but they would not visit with us or know our children. Mama held her face tight and resolute as she told me.

"Remember, our dearest daughter," she said to me, "I will live in thoughts of you. I will bless you and your children in every prayer I make. But Papa will not permit me to see you again." I saw the tears fall from her sad eyes.

"He gave permission for this marriage," I protested. "How can he be so cruel?"

She answered, "He is not cruel. He is obeying the Essene law. He knew you would suffer if you married Malach in the cloister, and so he gave you permission to marry outside of it." Then she said, "You have made it hard for yourself. You could have been part of our family here and lived with a good man, but you ruined it."

Mama's beautiful face, her soft, sad brown eyes, the high cheekbones shadowing the thinness of her chiseled features, have stayed forever etched into my brain. I see her now as she was then, the joy of life frozen in her love for Papa. Never to see her again.

"No," I cried. "Let me visit you. Let me bring my children to you. Why are you so hard on yourself and on me?"

Papa heard me and walked out of the room. I hugged my mother to me. We said nothing. Our silence spoke as if we had. Mama! I could not imagine life without her. I could not believe she would not come to see me and visit her grandchildren when we had them. What pleasure we would have walking the pathways surrounding our house, sewing and weaving, cooking with new kinds of herbs.

But I never saw her again. She died, the rabbi told me, when my daughter, Mary, was seven. Papa's blessings must have been given to me, though, because I was blessed beyond my dreams.

Ezekiel told me later what his father, Laban, said when Ezekiel said he wanted to marry me. "Are you crazy? You need to marry a woman of substance, with land and cattle. This girl will have nothing. Rabbis own nothing. He can give you nothing. I hear the daughter is a stubborn, willful woman. She was excommunicated."

Ezekiel answered, "If I cannot marry this girl, I will leave this country. You will never see me again."

Laban then agreed to the marriage and gave us our house as a start.

The celebration began at noon with wine and cheeses and fruits of all kind and left us exhausted. The rabbi blessed us. Then we made our way to an inn. A room had been cleaned, prepared, and covered with flowers and fruit and with blessings on the walls. We must consummate our marriage, be bonded, before the rabbi could bless us as one.

Now, in this room, my husband spoke to me, his bride, with love and promises of love to come, his eyes soft and warm. He took my hand in his and, looking into my eyes, quoted from the words of King Solomon:

"Set me as a seal upon thine heart, as a seal upon thine arm; for love is strong as death; jealousy is cruel as the grave; the coals thereof are coals of fire, which hath a most vehement flame.

"Many waters cannot quench love, neither can the floods drown it; if a man would give all the substance of his house for love, it would utterly be condemned."

After those words, we both drowned in our bliss. We bonded there in that room in a beautiful ceremony Ezekiel planned for us, hidden from all eyes.

We came back to the celebration. The village people sang and ate while the rabbi blessed us once again. Then, with questioning about our suitability to each other, he pronounced us to be one for all the years of our lives.

The house and land Laban bought for us had been abandoned for years. Ezekiel worked the land. He was outside at dawn to witness the glorious sunrise with prayer, and he was still there working when the skies blazed with fire at sunset. Together we spent long hours of joy, cleaning and repairing cracks in the old house, reveling in each other and the lack of other people's rules.

We replaced the loose, crumbling stones on the outside of the house. Nobody could say how old it was because nobody could remember when it wasn't there, or when it was last occupied. The rooms gave us much more space than an average house. We had a room for a child, if we had one, and another for weaving and sewing. We had our bedroom and a small kitchen space with a room where we could eat our meals. Open windows filtered light. At night we locked our windows with shutters boarded from inside. We worried that hungry animals from the hills might come in.

Ezekiel scrubbed and oiled an old wood table left in the house. We sealed the floors with heavy glue combined with dirt, which dried into a hard veneer. The mixture required a long drying time but proved to be a good tight surface, hard and clean. These floors held for our lifetime.

Every time we opened our front door, we marveled at the beauty surrounding us, the lush growth of trees and bushes, the rocks and hills, the glorious sunsets and sunrises, for we rose with the sun and often went to sleep not long after sunset.

Ezekiel piled stones high around the land near our house. "To shield us from the wind," he said. But I thought it defined our space. Three small carpets had been left in the house. We took them outside and beat them until their beautiful reds and blues and purples came alive. These small carpets gave me tremendous pride. I felt as if I were wealthy.

A young bride is the beloved of her husband and basks in his tenderness and ardor. It was for us a state of bliss. The two of us shared ourselves as one. "We must stay like this forever," I whispered to Ezekiel again and again. And Ezekiel always responded, "You are my beloved for all of my life." His arms went around me, our bodies blending into one, our lips pressing together. No woman ever felt more loved. In a world of repression, domination, and cruelty, we were on a little island, apart from the rest of the world.

We had a great deal of love in between working on our house, and soon I realized that I had not received my time. I told my husband that we could expect a child.

"That is as it should be," Ezekiel said. "We will have a family." I mused on the miracle that two people, when brought together, created one. And now we would be three.

I was to become a mother. A baby would come from the seed implanted in my body just as fruit carried the seed of its own renewal. It would be a seed of deep love and devotion.

The midwife came for the birthing. "For a firstborn," she advised, "it is better to have no one listening." With a smile coming from her lips and eyes, she shooed Ezekiel away, waving at him with her apron. She stayed with me through the rhythms of the birth movement until they brought out the baby. Then she put my infant on my stomach. The newborn lay there sleeping while I saw how beautifully formed she was, with large eyes and a sweet mouth.

"Mary is the image of her mother," Ezekiel insisted when he was allowed back to see his daughter. "The same white skin, and look at her eyes! She has a perfect face. I can see a sweet smile coming from her when she recognizes who she is and where she is." He picked her up to compare us.

"Her eyes are blue. Mine are brown. We have no blue eyes in our family. Do you have in yours?"

I answered, smiling, "I believe she is the image of my mother and has her beautiful face."

"That is strange," he said. "We don't have anyone with blue eyes in my family."

Mary was the image of my mother, more beautiful than anyone I had ever seen. When she grew a little older, our baby's smile seemed to light up as if she knew she was to be the happiest person on earth. This pleased both of us because we did not know how to act otherwise than to be as happy as our daughter. We worried that she was too pure and sweet and beautiful. She would be taken from us because we were not worthy of such a gift of love and beauty. But this did not happen.

Mary grew into a little girl with enormous eyes of gray blue and a perfect oval face. Her lips turned up with a perpetual look of a secret smile, a mouth I thought was more her father's than my mother's.

"Tell me the story about how you and Papa met," my daughter liked to ask when as a little girl she scrambled into my lap. She asked for the story so many times I grew sick of it. But I would tell her because she got so much pleasure from it.

"One day," I began, "my papa was away in the desert praying, because he was a very religious man and a rabbi. I begged my mother to let me stay the night with my friend, Rebecca, away from the Essene caves where we lived. Rebecca lived in

Bethlehem, our village. We liked to be together to dream of the time when we would be married and have children of our own." I hugged Mary tight to let her know how much I loved her. She smiled back. She loved to hear this story.

"Rebecca and I passed through our village to draw water at the well. That is when I first saw your father. My eyes opened wide because I thought I knew him, but I didn't. He was a stranger. You know what happened?" I asked my daughter.

She giggled. "A thousand lights went on. Your head buzzed. He turned to stare at you."

"Why should I tell you this story? You already know it," I teased Mary. She kissed me. "More, Mama, please."

"I saw your father another time when Rebecca and I were drawing water. Rebecca and I agreed a long time before that your father was very handsome. He came up to me, smiling. I trembled and dropped my bucket of water, spilling it all over the sand. I could only keep my face hidden by looking down."

I tilted my daughter's face toward me. "Now tell me what your father said to me."

Mary answered, "You are the beautiful girl of my dreams. What is your name?"

"And what did I do?" I asked her.

"It was forbidden for you to talk to a stranger, so you left your bucket and ran away," the little angel said with a flourish of her hands. Then she slipped off my lap and went outside to visit her friends: a goat, a sheep, and a little newborn lamb she had a special affection for.

Ezekiel loved his daughter with a deep feeling especially for her. It pleased me because Papa had seemed so indifferent in his love for me. Yet I did not feel that Ezekiel loved me less.

"You are my soul," he liked to say as he put his arms

around me. I could not answer even though my pulse raced. I was taught that husbands were not supposed to show affection to their wives, and so I pulled away, too shy for such an ardent man. But Ezekiel paid no attention to my ways. He reached for me and embraced me until I dissolved into a puddle of bliss, as I always did and had from the beginning of our marriage. We were in paradise.

"We'll never leave this place. Promise me," I begged Ezekiel. "God has given us heaven. I want to grow old here with my children, and I want to be with you until we are like two old oak trees growing together."

I thought of the beauty of this country, of Bethlehem, our village, bordered by hills and near the Sea of Galilee; of red sunsets, the golden glow in the sky; of the apricot trees and fig trees and singing birds flying in patterns across our blue sky with soft winds pressing against my cheeks. Nature cupped us in her hands and placed us in a bowl of joy to live out our lives with her.

"I promise," Ezekiel said. He took me in his arms. "We will live in this very house for all of our lives."

"We will never leave Bethlehem," I whispered.

How warm it was to live in the arms of a man of God who had never been cruel to humans or to animals. Ezekiel disapproved of my way of discouraging wild animals from coming close to our house. I found a long, heavy stick to hit them with if they would not leave with a shout.

My husband told me I did not need to hit them. He said I was to listen to them and hear their cries, which told of their need for food or a mate, or others of their own kind to be around when they were lost. Soon I could hear the difference in their cries and discriminate between an animal in trouble and one with an empty belly. If the animal was hungry, I brought some bread or lamb or any scraps left from a meal, and put it outside our land so that the animal could eat it after we removed ourselves into our house.

Animals of all kinds roamed the hills: fox, little rabbits, large wolves, strong leopards, and bears, of course. Yes, I was most afraid of the leopards. They leaped and prowled and could climb a tree in a second. I was afraid of them, but Ezekiel was not. He and Mary walked through the hills without carrying a stick or any other protection for themselves. "They know you are God's blessed," I said. "But I don't feel that way. I feel safer with a good stout stick to use if it proves necessary."

As Mary grew a little older, she seemed to become part of the nature surrounding her. She knew the names of the trees on our land: shady cedars, pine, the flowering acacias, date palms, poplar and the shittah tree, oak as well as fruit trees bearing apricots and pears, apples and pomegranates, figs and olives. Mary talked to the trees as if they were alive.

"They do live, Mama," she informed me. "I feel so bad because they cannot move. But they can think and they know they are protecting the birds and animals who come to them."

Mary sent many prayers of love into them. Our child questioned Ezekiel about the plants and trees she saw when they walked in the hills. Ezekiel knew all about plants because he had spent his life among them. Now he could tell Mary that a plant grew so tall and gave off certain herbs and that a tree would only bear fruit if there were a male and female tree to blend. He taught her many things about the life of animals—

how they were born and how they suffered from lack of attention on the part of their owners. He showed her his love and respect for wild animals as well as his love and respect for those in husbandry. Ezekiel took Mary with him on his walks in the hills. He looked for suffering animals whatever the cause, and when he could, he helped them.

Mary sat with us one evening as we watched the drama of the changing colors of the sky. The colors, apricot and orange, white and blue, and rays of bright red, reminded her that this earth was created by a power far beyond ours.

"Tell me about God," she said. "Was he a man? Did he have children? How many kind of gods were there? Did God ever talk to people? Why did God make people different from the way he was so that they had to pray to him? Why didn't he make them the right way in the beginning?"

"Child," I answered. "You don't need to think about these things. God loves you. You are very special to him. He hears you, and he keeps you close to him."

"I know that," Mary said. "I talk to him all the time, but he doesn't answer my questions. He acts as if I am his daughter who must just listen to him in silence."

I thought her answer strange. Just listen to him in silence: that is what a rabbi might say. Mary was only eight. Where did these conversations come from?

I did not know how to answer. Neither did Ezekiel.

"What can we explain about God if God doesn't want to explain who he is? It is enough to know God loves you," Ezekiel finally answered.

"I love him with all my heart," Mary said, doing a little skip with her feet that took her away from us and to the front door. "But I wish he'd talk to me." She left.

"Wait until she asks about angels and demons and spirits," Ezekiel reminded me, smiling. "How do we explain those?"

We believed what was generally thought to be true. Spirit beings, both good and bad, existed. We paid little attention to such beliefs and had no dealings with devils or angels.

"Let us be as we are forever," I said again and again. I even prayed.

"Those who believe in angels and devils create them from their minds, don't they?" I asked Ezekiel, hoping for confirmation. He sat with me while he repaired a rope of linen. He smiled and nodded.

So I went on with my philosophy. "I believe angels who minister to us on earth are created out of the love we feel within ourselves, and the devils are the angry forces from our human selves. These are released in angelic or demonic actions. Forces created out of anger must return to the sender with double force. That is why angry people create demonic situations for themselves."

"That's a long speech," my husband remarked. "I believe the same thing. So it must be true." He looked at me with such fondness that I got up and left the room. It was not the right time for lovemaking.

Some days Rebecca came to visit. We met at the well often, but our purest joy was when we sat together twining threads and revealing our secrets to each other. Rebecca told me she had fallen in love with a Samaritan, a gentile of great wealth and education who had stopped at the well for water one afternoon. When she told her father, he said, "If you should marry such a person, a man uncircumcised and without respect for the laws of Moses, I will kill him and you. It is forbidden. You may not marry him, not even if he declares himself a Hebrew." It was also forbidden for an unmarried virgin to talk to a married woman, I reminded myself.

Rebecca's father went to Jerusalem to consult a rabbi and find her a proper husband. Rebecca bowed to his demands. "I have no choice," she said. "He really would kill us, because he could not live with such disgrace."

"Maybe you will like the man your father chooses," I said, trying to console her with my words, but I knew she would not find her love again. Love does not flow everywhere. But when it is truly known, nothing should deny it life. I did not tell her that.

I did not tell Mary that either, but I didn't have to. Her understanding of life was already profound. I tried to make her life one of love and peace, but she did not want to have such a life.

Mary wanted to live her own life and bear her own sorrows, if they were to come. Our child was born with a strong and powerful ability to withstand suffering. This did not mean she couldn't or wouldn't feel the suffering of others.

Like Ezekiel, Mary had a gift of healing in a different way. We thought she was given a gift from God. Our daughter talked with the animals, our goat, the sheep, the lambs and little animals in the hills, the rabbits, the squirrels, our cat, and even wild animals.

When she saw a sick creature hiding from the others, she asked God to heal it, and it would scamper away healed, my husband claimed.

I saw Mary many times take a bird fallen from its nest and place it in a similar nest she had made out of twigs and leaves. Then she would talk to it in soft tones, passing her hand over the nest. The bird would recover and fly away.

She did chores while singing in a loud voice all the little ditties her father had taught her. She liked to sing. I said I thought she had a beautiful voice, but her father said, "You would say that if she cackled like a hen or crowed like a rooster. I think you are right. She has a beautiful voice but you do not need to envy it. You have a beautiful voice yourself."

Mary never had any sisters or brothers. That was the sad fact of our lives. We tried to have other children because God said, "Be fruitful and multiply," but we were not successful. Mary told us not to worry and for me to stop using charms and prayers to get them.

"God has his purposes in not giving you other children," my daughter told me. I thought these were wise words and stopped worrying.

"But will Mary ever give us grandchildren?" I asked Ezekiel. "It would be a blight on our lives if we did not have grandchildren."

When Mary finished her chores—feeding the animals, combing the silky wool for weaving, helping me in the kitchen—she would run toward the hills she loved. Even when Mary was almost sixteen years old, she never turned dreamy the way Rebecca and I did. She never talked about the future she would have when she found a husband.

One day I started for the village to buy some scented oil for Mary to use on her body. On the path I felt a chill, as if something had happened to Mary. I shivered and could not talk, but stood spellbound in the street. Then I realized what I was doing and returned to our house. Ezekiel didn't notice how upset I was. I didn't want to say anything because he wouldn't have wanted me to go into the hills alone. What if we found our daughter happily singing to the birds? I would feel foolish, and he might think I had become overconcerned about our daughter. I threw a shawl over my head and hurried out of the door to look for Mary myself.

I searched in all the places where she usually could be found. "Mary. Mary. Where are you, my daughter?" I called her name until my voice gave out, but she did not appear. Then, tired and hungry, but still very concerned, I returned to the house. Ezekiel was waiting for me, concerned that I had not returned home.

"I can't find Mary," I told him. "She is not in any of the places she usually goes to. I went to the Tree of God. That child always goes there when she wants to talk to God. I went down a hill into the woods calling her name, but she did not answer. I am so worried. What can have happened to her?"

"We'll try again," he said as he started for the hills with me. "Let's call out her name. She must have forgotten time." Ezekiel roared out her name. "MARY, where are you?" His words echoed in the hills.

The sun promised to hide in half an hour. Then it would be dark. "We should not let her run in the hills by herself," I said. "Mary is the prey of any evil person walking there." These words came too late, I feared, trembling from exhaustion and worry.

"Don't fret, my heart," my husband comforted me. "Mary can take good care of herself. She will be home soon, and she will tell you where she was, as she always does."

I had a premonition that something was happening to her. But what? "Where is she? What do we do now?"

"Go home," Ezekiel said. "Maybe she is already there, but if not, I'm sure she knows the way, even in the dark."

The sky had darkened by the time we reached our house. Mary had not come back. I was more worried than ever.

"She will be home very soon," Ezekiel said. He was right. Mary arrived soon after we did. Instead of bursting with enthusiasm to tell us of her adventures, she went into her room and lay down and closed her eyes. This alarmed me more because it was not like Mary to do this.

"Mary, my own daughter, why are you so quiet? Where were you? It is very late."

"Mama, I'm tired. I would like to go to sleep."

Ezekiel spoke. "We want to know where you have been. We have been very worried that you suffered some harm in those hills."

Mary lay on her bed, her eyes bright and her face radiant.

"I know something happened to you, Mary. Please tell us, the way you always do. What happened to you this afternoon? We will not be angry with you." I caressed her forehead. She looked at her father and agreed by nodding her head.

I saw some brush or sand in her hair. I saw she was weary beyond words. Should Mary wait till morning to tell us what happened so that she could sleep now? I signaled Ezekiel, "Should we wait until tomorrow to question our daughter?"

He read my mind and shook his head, "No." He left us alone, Mary and me, so that our daughter could speak more freely about her experience.

CHAPTER II

CONCEPTION

I washed Mary's face and combed her hair and bathed her body as she lay on her bed, aware that there was blood on her undergarment. It was pure, that body. I could tell by its response to me under my hands. There was no shrinking of that white flesh, lovely and rosy as ever, in fact, more so. Light seemed to emblazon her body, and I could feel her power as if it were singing around her. I knew she had done no wrong. Perhaps the blood came from a scratch. I did not see one, but her dress was torn from the rocks and the brambles she encountered when she went to the cave. My daughter had been taken, but I didn't want to believe it. She gave no sign of guilt or shame or fear. She was as radiant as ever.

"I love you, Mother," she said. "I have spoken with the angels Gabriel and Michael. Raphael, too, has come to me. I have been told such strange things. I cannot believe them, but they are true, even if I can't fathom them. I am to become the mother of the Savior of the world. I am to be his mother on earth. I was told my role would be as important as his because I would carry within me the strong love of God the child would be wrapped in."

She looked up at me, her long black hair streaming around the bed, her eyes shining with a light of joy, and her slender reed of a body resting without a sign of suffering, of being exploited or used for evil.

"My child, my child!" I answered, finding it hard to believe what I was hearing. "You sound demented. What happened? Where were you? Who came to you? Tell me the truth. Why are you so happy? You have been taken. The evidence is here." I refused to let myself believe what my daughter had told me.

"You will have a child. You are only sixteen and you are not married." Tears gathered in my eyes as I thought of the horror this would bring upon the family. In my mind, I saw the village gathering with stones to throw at Mary, for that was the punishment inflicted upon any woman who dared defy the law and lay with a man not her husband. The law of our Essene sect required that the bride be bonded with her husband at the wedding ceremony and that she acknowledge herself as his property, to obey him as he saw fit.

It was the village women in their long dresses with shawls over their shaven heads who would inflict the punishment. None can be as cruel as those who are themselves held in a vice of suffering. For most women did suffer lives of unbelievable torment because their husbands and sons treated them as useful instruments for their needs.

Mary smiled up at me. "You are right, Mother. I will have the most wonderful son ever to be born. That's what I was told." Her eyes were as bright as the stars.

"The voice said to me, 'There is a cave behind where you stand. A large mulberry bush hides it, but you will find it. Go into that cave and then you can sleep, for you are to become the mother of the Messiah. You are to be honored above all women because you are a holy woman of God through your blood and through the power of love that envelops your body and your heart.'

"I found the cave and went inside. A strange warm light filled the room. I rested against a wall and fell asleep. There was a dream, or perhaps it was real. I know it was real, but then, I was asleep. I dreamed the angel Michael came over me. I was enveloped in peace, in beauty, in love, in a place of enchantment so powerful that I must have fainted. I smelled sandalwood. I love the scent of sandalwood. The scent is pure.

"Mother, you cannot know how filled I was with light and joy. My Mother, there was another angel standing there, Gabriel. He stood, watching Michael and holding his hands over me. Michael and Gabriel. Were there others? I don't know. I opened my eyes to hear Gabriel speak. He said, 'Daughter, you have been impregnated with the Messiah. Your spirit is entwined with that of the child. The child will be flesh and blood of your flesh and blood and that of Abraham's seed in Ezekiel.

"'We will not forsake you ever. You have only to call and we will answer you. You will be the light to guide this child to his destiny for he is to change the consciousness of the world and leave his heart for all men to cry and pray to. He shall be named Jeschu, and he shall lead his people through the teachings of a master who guides him from within.'"

I had heard enough. My daughter was ranting. Fantasies were filling her brain like little demons playing with her thoughts.

My head pounded. "Hush, Mary, sleep. I have heard enough. Let's see what you say tomorrow."

She fell asleep, one arm curled over her shiny dark hair and the other flung out across the bed, feet sprawled in a childlike fashion. She was a child, an angel, I thought, barely sixteen, barely awake to life beyond these walls.

Ezekiel and I held no secrets. In trouble we became closer, not hidden from each other. So I came to him and told him what Mary said and what I had seen. "Our daughter has been taken in the hills, but I don't know how it happened." I didn't believe Mary's story. Neither did Ezekiel credit it. Not that we thought our child would lie to us. She believed what she said.

"Mary is suffering from shock," he said. "Someone has harmed her. We must talk to our rabbi."

My husband left for the rabbi's place just a few houses away. I waited at the door for him to return, looking to see if anyone would hear or recognize Ezekiel and wonder why he went for the rabbi at night. But I saw that all the houses were dark. When darkness comes, our village people go to bed until daylight awakens them to a new day. I hoped no one would know we saw the rabbi, for that would stir up curiosity.

The stars are magnificent in the night, so bright and alive in their beauty. They protect our world with a brilliant blanket of light. The stars are fixed for us. They are always with us and are a part of our lives as much as food. There is no way we could live without the stars because they have within them the light of God and can be trusted to guide us. They are the light of heaven and the light of God. We see the stars as being our own light and the way to God. So we look to them for our comfort and for our love from God who gives it to us through the aura of his own light. These were my thoughts as I stood there taking in the wonder of the stars.

I waited outside the door for Ezekiel's return, holding one hand onto the edge in case I needed to retreat from some animal running out of the hills. Wind rustled the trees. Frogs and crickets in the background gave their usual mating call in chorus. I let myself feel trust for whatever happened, as Abraham did when he brought Isaac to the mountain as a sacrifice. The moon, brighter than usual, also streamed its light to my door as if to comfort me.

What did I know of this world? Were there really angels around us? Our writings spoke of Gabriel and Michael and other angels, but I had no knowledge of them.

People in the village believed in evil spirits disguised as animals and in angels and strange gods. Hebrews considered the villagers, mostly Samaritans, to be impure and ignorant because they believed in false gods. I often spoke to these people as neighbors, but I did not know their ways or their thoughts. We helped them if we heard a baby lamb bleating because it was lost or if there was not enough water in their well.

I recognized Ezekiel's steps as he walked back toward our house. Rabbi Kahane came with him. This was an honor, for the rabbi seldom visited a house.

I hurried back inside to prepare for our guest. I brought the light of the stars into the house with candles. I took out cups and brought wine to put on the table in front of the men. I did not sit with them but stayed in a corner away from them, as a wife is expected to do. Ezekiel motioned me to come to the table and then I did.

We are not allowed to keep secrets from our rabbi, and so we told him about the blood on Mary's undergarment and what Mary had dreamed. The rabbi rubbed his beard, an exceptionally long, black one. A short, rounded man, his black hair reaching to his shoulder, the holy teacher resembled other holy men from Jerusalem who sit all day in prayer when they visit the cloister where my parents live.

Ezekiel and I watched the rabbi sip his wine and waited for him to talk. Finally he cleared his throat. His hands flew in the air in gestures of despair as he talked. "Maybe a magician did it. They walk the hills."

There was no question in his mind about whether Mary had chosen to lay with a boy. He had known her since birth. Often the holy man spoke to Ezekiel in admiration of our daughter. "She will be a blessing to you," he would say. We joked about his words between us because he repeated himself so many times. She was already a blessing to us.

The rabbi had nothing more to say to us. He covered his head with a cape against the night air and turned as he reached the door. "She must be married. We must find her a husband who will understand what has happened."

Ezekiel turned red after the rabbi left, thinking about his words.

"Mary married? That innocent child? She will never be like other women. Her soul and heart are very special. What man could give her the understanding and love we could?" he lamented.

"But," I said, remembering what happened to Adiela, who had been stoned to death when her husband found her with a lover, "we cannot leave her to the gossip and judgment of this village even if we could get our own people to accept what happened. The village people will taunt her. There are those in our own sect who would condemn her and not believe her story."

I lay in bed next to Ezekiel's warm body, but I could not sleep. Mary's innocence was so beautiful because she had more than the innocence of a child. She trusted life. What frightened a child did not shake her. Once, walking on a path, we saw a man walking alongside a team of oxen pulling a cart loaded with cut wood. The wood was piled too high. and the load slid off the cart, toppling on him. The cart and the heavy bodied oxen pulled away, dragging the man until he was dead.

Watching this, we screamed and stayed away from him. But Mary ran to him after the oxen were stopped and put her hand on what had been his forehead. I pulled her away, his blood on her hand, but she just said, "Mama, I asked God to keep him safe."

Mary, my baby, had been taken as a woman. Thank God she didn't remember what had happened to her. Then I wondered whether she would have been frightened anyway.

But what if this were the will of God? What if Mary had been an instrument of his will, and the archangel Michael had put the spirit of God in her body and then brought in another angel in the form of a man to plant his seed? Such a man, chosen by God, would have been so pure and holy that he would hardly touch her. Still, he would have to plant the seed. In that case, she would bear a spirit-man, the like of which could shake the earth and cause it to tremble in awe for all time to come.

Mary woke the next morning as happy and lively as always. She did not mention the dream or what had happened to her. I said nothing. But when she started for her usual mountain wanderings, I stopped her.

"You will stay with me," I said. "You are too old to wander in the hills alone."

The only way we could remove the stigma of a baby was through a marriage. Otherwise, how could we explain this birth to the world? If I were to say our daughter has been chosen to give birth to the Messiah, we would be stoned to death for blasphemy.

Ezekiel said he would try to find a man who would marry Mary and claim the child as his own.

Mary insisted, "This is not necessary, Mother. I will be taken care of by Michael and Gabriel because I will be the mother of the Messiah."

Ezekiel said he would not hear of it. The village was sure to stone her to death the minute they learned she was pregnant but without a husband. "If you tell them you are to become the mother of the Messiah, they will laugh and sneer and then kill you."

Mary said, "Father, let me suffer if I must, but do not insist that I marry, because if you do, and I do marry a man, I will not be with him as a wife."

This upset us both. What were we to do? We asked the rabbi to come to our house again and give us some of his wisdom.

The rabbi came the next day to talk with Mary. His warm, understanding eyes told me he loved her. I thanked God for that. They looked each other in the eye: the one with the innocent eyes and the rabbi, a holy teacher, with searching brown ones.

He said to her, "Beloved child, do not believe you can live in this village without a husband, and if you do marry, you are obliged to be a wife in every way."

Mary responded with a smile.

"Is it possible," Ezekiel wanted to know, "that the story Mary tells is true, that she saw the real archangel, Michael, and that she is to become the mother of the Messiah?"

I felt my husband's pain as he continued.

"If she is to be the mother of a messiah, isn't it possible she will be protected from death? Would a woman with the Messiah waiting to be born in her body be subject to death? How, then, would the Messiah be born?"

The rabbi rubbed his beard some more and cocked his head to one side. "It is possible. A messiah is due. Mary knows nothing of messiahs. I know she is an innocent child. She did not commit a forbidden act. It is possible that she is to bear the Messiah. It is also possible that the magician was an instrument of God. Such are his ways. We cannot know them."

"It is possible that she will not become pregnant," I said. "It is possible he just put the story in her head." I was worried that if Mary had lost her purity, she could no longer be considered for marriage by any Hebrew, and I would never know the pleasure of my grandchildren.

"She is pregnant," the rabbi said. "I know it already."

"Then what are we to do?" Ezekiel asked, as if the rabbi could pull an answer out of the earth like a vegetable.

The rabbi asked Mary to repeat to him exactly what had happened. Then he asked, "Are you sure you were asleep when this happened? Are you sure it was a dream?"

Mary answered, "I don't know. This is the way I thought it was. I saw the angels, but maybe I wasn't asleep. I don't know. I can't tell."

The rabbi rubbed his long black beard. "She's been taken," he told us. "The man who came into the cave must have had magic powers. He first made the angels appear, and then he put her in a trance."

"Are there such magicians?" I asked.

"Yes," said the rabbi. "They wander everywhere. They know magic from Egypt and secret teachings that are forbidden. They are evil foes of God and of the Hebrew people. They would destroy the Hebrews, for the Hebrews teach the laws of Jehovah while they believe in the laws of nature and that man controls the destiny of nature." The rabbi said he would think about our problem and left.

The whole world went upside down for us. We could not think of letting our daughter sacrifice her life for a baby even though it would be the Messiah. We had no way of knowing if that were true or if she had been taken by a magician, as the rabbi suggested. Could someone wandering in the hills hypnotize her and fill her head with the idea that she would bear the Messiah?

The only solution was to have her marry but not honor her vows and then leave her husband. But who would agree to that? We talked and talked about the men eligible for marriage. Eventually the rabbi was won over to our way of thinking.

We called him over to discuss potential husbands for Mary. After some thinking his face lit up with a smile. "Ah, a possibility! His arms shot up in the air expressing his pleasure, his brown eyes shining. "Joseph, a fine man. His wife died and left him with three young boys."

"You know him?" the holy man asked Ezekiel and, not waiting for an answer, said, "This man is a scholar and highly respected. He lives in Nazareth. I can talk to him. Maybe he will agree to marry Mary and not expect her to be his mate. He is already a man without a wife."

Ezekiel knew Joseph. "Yes. He would be a good man, and he would never talk. He is also an excellent carpenter." Ezekiel smiled a little bit. "He acts as if he is very pleased with his life. But how can he be, when he lives alone?"

The rabbi went to see Joseph, to explain what had happened. Then he returned to our house. I could see disappointment in his eyes.

"It is not so good. He says it would be living a lie to pretend." The rabbi paused to think about it. "He is right, unless it is in God's plan. If it is intended, then it will happen. He will marry the child."

We were very sad and wished we could persuade Joseph to do what the rabbi asked, but we said no more.

A few days later, Joseph came to the door. Mary was away and Ezekiel was working in a field. He found me preparing a soup for our evening meal. I wiped my hands. "Ezekiel is not here and Mary is away," I told him. "But come in for tea."

What a handsome man, I thought, judging him to be about thirty. It's a pity he lost his wife when he has three boys to care for.

I sat with him, waiting for him to say why he came. He sipped his tea slowly but finally put his cup down and said. "I had a dream last night, a very strange one. I don't know what to think of it."

Joseph went silent, and I waited. I did admire him. I liked his strong, muscular arms and the leanness of his body. Joseph wore the Essene beard, long and uncut.

He spoke again as if he had never paused. "In this dream I was told by the archangel Michael to protect Mary, as she was to be a virgin mother, a holy woman, who is to beget the Messiah."

"She is to be the feminine counterpart of the Messiah. So, I have come here to tell you it is my honor to marry your daughter. She shall have complete protection for her lifetime if she chooses it."

"Let's tell Ezekiel right away," I said excitedly. Mary had told the truth. Joseph's story seemed to me to be a miracle verifying hers. She would bear the Messiah. There was no magician. All would be well.

We went together into the fields and told my husband we could plan the wedding with his permission. Mary came home.

"That is good, Mother," she said. "Now you won't worry anymore."

We set the wedding within two weeks. It was a very merry wedding with wine and all kinds of prepared dishes of herbs and vegetables, olives, carrots with honey, eggplants and delicious lamb, cake and fruits, apricots, pears, oranges, and the finest ripe red grapes.

We gave the young couple many presents of food and fowl, wheat, and other grains. We could not afford to do this, but we were so grateful we didn't care.

Mary blossomed with her pregnancy, never sick or cross, still singing the little ditties her father taught her as she did her chores. She spent more and more time in the hills, although Joseph cautioned her, and I worried until she was safe at home again. Mary had no concern about herself. She knew she had a kind of protection we did not understand.

The hills were alive with all kinds of animals and plants, and it seemed we could never know them all. Fig trees, ancient as time, were plentiful wherever we walked. Pomegranate trees grew wild, offering us their delicious red fruit. Wild strawberries grew on vines following a tree to wrap around. Wildflowers grew in fields, coloring them into carpets. They blossomed in the spring when the entire hill territory came alive with new birth. We never knew when we would discover another kind of fruit, for there were new kinds coming out on bushes and vines that we never recognized before. We also ate richly from the fruits and the vegetables we grew, and from cereals we also grew barley and wheat and certain kinds of rye.

In the summer we often had violent storms. Lightning struck across the sky, threatening to break into our house and destroy us with its force. It came with cracks of thunder that could terrorize the strongest heart. We hid under our furniture when we knew this kind of storm was coming, for with it came strong winds that could blow away all we had. When the sky turned black as a vicious man's heart, the people in town knew there would be a storm of great proportion. The sky became our enemy, threatening our lives.

Sometimes we gathered in a cave dug into the earth and hid from the outside so that the storm could not see us and destroy us. We would wait inside in the stuffy, wet, humid air, breathing hard to get some kind of relief from our terror. The storm could blow for a long time before it gave itself up and went somewhere else to frighten others. We never knew why the storms came. They just seemed to be evil spirits getting back at us for having land and working as we did.

When the storms let up, we had time to reflect.

"What if he's a girl?" I asked Mary. She smiled as she watched me card wool.

"He won't be," she answered.

"You can't know that," I argued.

She wouldn't answer. That was Mary. Once she made her statement, she wouldn't argue. On the other hand, she never got angry if you argued. She listened. If you were right, she would say she was sorry. But if she didn't think so, she would say nothing. That's the way she was about going into the hills.

I kept saying, "Mary, stay out of the hills. Do you want the same thing to happen to you again?" She would answer, "No." Without being defiant, she would not listen to me. But nothing happened.

I watched her belly get bigger and bigger. Our neighbors congratulated us on such a quick pregnancy. We had a fertile daughter and that was a blessing. She would have many strong sons we were told, for Joseph was a strong man.

Then one day, a few months before she was due to have the baby, Mary came in and told me the angel Michael had spoken to her again. He said her baby would be delivered normally without any severe suffering, that she would have a boy, and that she was to call him Jeschu. He said the angels of heaven were well pleased with her. She was the bearer of a God child who would bring holy teachings to mankind. His teachings would change the course of the world.

Mary told me this without being at all dramatic. It seemed matter of course with her.

"The angel Michael will take care of me," she assured me. "And I am to be the mother of the Messiah." I couldn't help remarking he hadn't done much to save her from the disgrace she would have suffered if we hadn't found her a husband.

She smiled. "He knew what you would do. He knew you would always protect me."

About two months before her delivery time, Mary seemed to burst with energy. She cleaned her cottage and then came to mine to help me. She danced around because she couldn't keep still.

We awaited the birth of the child as if Joseph were his father. This lie gave us sadness as we were not accustomed to pretending, especially not to each other. If we told people our daughter had been embraced by an archangel and was carrying the Messiah, we would have been laughed out of our village.

The baby was born in our house in Bethlehem on the twelfth day of Tischri or September. I was there with Mary. My grandson gave his first cry like any normal baby when he arrived. Mary had the best help we could give her. Joseph, too, stayed at our house. He took the baby in his arms as if he had given life to it, as if the child were his own. He was just as joyful. We were so grateful to him that I cried. Ezekiel brought him two of our best laying hens as a gift.

Only one unusual thing happened. After the cord was cut and Jeschu was washed and brought to his mother, who laid him on her stomach, he lifted his head, looked around at us, and smiled. "Look!" I said to Mary. "It's a sign. I've never seen a newborn baby do that."

Soon after Jeschu was born, Joseph came to our house at sunset. A soft breeze blew across the land. Autumn wind and autumn skies promised an early fall. It was the time of day to rest and savor the blessings of a day's labor done.

I welcomed our new son-in-law when he came alone without Mary. I beckoned him to sit. As usual, he was silent until everything settled down. Then, in his soft voice he said, "I must go to Jerusalem to be counted in the census and to pay taxes. I would like for Mary and the baby to go with me. She will meet my family, and we will stay in Jerusalem where I can find work until she is strong enough to come back here."

"But your boys. Will you take them, too?"

"No. Their grandmother and grandfather will keep them. They are well provided for. I cannot take them away."

"From your wife's mother and father?"

Joseph nodded. He looked sad for a moment. I knew he was remembering his wife. "Yes, they have become the parents to these boys, and I would not take them away from them."

"Joseph, don't you think it is too soon for Mary to travel? She could stay here with Jeschu. The baby is so young."

Just then Mary walked into the house with her son. Joseph looked at her. "Would you like to come with me to Jerusalem? You won't have to walk. We'll take the donkey for you and the baby to ride."

Mary turned to me. "I feel very good, Mama. I want to go."

Joseph asked nothing of my daughter. I could see that he loved and cared about her. He would not let harm come to her. I worried for other reasons. She was still not purified. The purification consisted of baths and rituals and prayers once her blood stopped flowing. That is what worried me. Riding on the donkey could cause her to hemorrhage. I pictured her riding out for a few miles and then being taken off the donkey because she was bleeding. There she would die by the side of the road.

By now Ezekiel had come in from the hot fields with sweaty beads forming on his face. He stood there listening to us. When Mary and Joseph left, he comforted me by taking me in his arms.

"What can we do?" he asked. "She is a married woman and under the authority of her husband."

"I shall miss her so," I said. "She is still a baby. I can't let her go." The tears rolled in drops down my face.

"I promised you, my dearest soul, that we would never leave our house. It is you who begged for that promise. Now do you want us to break it? Do you want to leave here and go to Jerusalem with our daughter and her husband?"

I couldn't answer. No, I didn't want to leave the love flowing in our house. But I didn't want to be separated from our daughter, either. She needed me. She could become ill with an infection or a cold, or the baby could have a fever. I had natural remedies. Joseph would not know what to do.

"We must go," I said, drying my tears and trying for a smile. "But not for long." I never dreamed it would be more than sixteen years before we returned.

I prepared for the trip with extreme care, for it was nearing winter and we would need warm clothes, especially for evening, while the heat during the day would burn us. We took the mule and loaded him as high as we dared with provisions. I packed oil and all kinds of dried food—cereals, sweet cakes, and fruits. We could buy food in the villages to prepare, but still there were things I wanted to bring myself. We would use vessels especially set aside for milk dishes. We did not mix meat dishes with milk dishes as that was against the law of Moses. We also needed candles for prayers and tefillin to wind about the arms and foreheads of the men for their special prayers.

"Mama, I know it is hard for you to leave Bethlehem, but I feel so much better to know you are coming with us," Mary told me. "I need you and want you near even though I feel strong enough to make this journey. And you and Papa are blessed for coming."

CHAPTER III

THE INN

Our journey to Jerusalem began in the chilly dawn. Leaves from the shittah trees blew around us, sometimes swirling and shifting under our feet. September's brisk air promised us relief from the summer heat. I gave thanks to God for that.

We made a long narrow procession, Joseph leading, while Mary sat upon a donkey, holding the tiny baby close to her heart. Then, after her, a mule loaded with blankets, food, and clothing. Ezekiel and I followed, leading mules loaded high with more food, blankets, clothing, and utensils.

The path went downward toward the Sea of Galilee. Even some distance away I could feel its power. The sea brought to the air strong feelings that sent chills through me, although I do not know why.

"Can you feel the difference in the atmosphere?" I asked Ezekiel. He nodded yes.

I watched my daughter for signs of fatigue. The baby was secure, tucked next to her breast. The rocking rhythm of the donkey kept him quiet. What would my grandson look like? Many people had commented on his blue eyes, blue as our blue sea and like Mary's, but he had a down of black hair and shadows of dark brows to come. His tiny body was slender like Mary's. What if he developed wings such as the archangels are supposed to have? So far, he had a normal boy's body.

King David must have had such blue eyes as our grandson. Could this child be King David returning to earth as predicted by Isaiah, the holy prophet of Israel? I shivered at the thought. I imagined David, his torment at being human and selfish and greedy, that poet's great soul forever yearning to be a true servant to his God, drugged by beauty and love, reaching for holiness, then plummeting into the lust of his body. The beautiful psalms he left us, his holiness, his evil—surely in David God had poured spirit into flesh, measure for measure.

Would young Jeschu be tormented between flesh and spirit like David and have to choose? There was time to think about such things as we made our way. Ezekiel never spoke about the origin of Jeschu. I had no one to talk to and discuss my fears.

"We must firmly say and believe that Jeschu is the son of Joseph and Mary. We know nothing else, we speak nothing else," he insisted.

Mary was an example of Abraham's faith. She didn't seem to give the miracle of conception a thought. She was certain that the future would unfold under the protection of her beloved archangels, Michael and Gabriel. For now, she accepted herself as the ordinary wife of an ordinary man.

I could not stop the thoughts running through my head. My daughter would be hurt and suffer because her child was different, marked by God for work I could not imagine. And the baby, such a beautiful baby, did he not look and act normal? What would happen to him? What destiny did he have as a messiah, if in fact he was to be a messiah, to our own Hebrew people?

I imagined a scene if Jeschu turned out to be the Messiah. I envisioned this precious baby as a grown man in robes of purple with gold threads, a gold crown atop his head, his feet encased in gold sandals, riding astride a splendid horse and bowing to throngs of worshipers as he moved through the cobblestone streets of Jerusalem. Bowers of roses and lilies scented the air, people tossed flowers to him and green leaves and wreaths scattered in his path. As he rode, those lining the streets bowed to him. "The Messiah! The Messiah!" They kissed his feet. They cried out for a blessing.

Ezekiel awakened me from my reverie to point out that our daughter's face had turned pale. We had walked no more than a few miles on a rocky path. She must stop and rest, drink a warm brew of herbs, and sleep. She should have waited a few more days before undertaking such a trip as this. I spoke to Joseph.

"We must stop," he agreed.

Joseph looked at me. "Don't be concerned, little Grandmother. If Mary wants to go back with you, of course, she will."

Mary said nothing. I knew she suffered pain because she was pale to the point of whiteness.

We made our way up a path to the house of our friends, Efron and Hannah. A stranger answered the door. Efron had died. His wife Hannah had moved to Jerusalem. We tried several places and even asked a holy man walking in the street if he knew of a place where we might stay the night, but he did not. He shrugged his shoulders.

"Many people are going to Jerusalem, like you. They stop here overnight. But there is an inn. Take this path down to the roadway."

I had forgotten about the old inn. We thanked the rabbi and wished him good health. Why, I wondered, are all holy men short with long beards, long hair, and white robes? Is it required? Did God create them out of one form so everyone would recognize a holy man?

A sharp wind came up, blowing dust over us. Joseph walked ahead to see if he could get rooms at the inn. Ezekiel took the reins of the donkey and the mule. I worried about my daughter.

"Give me the baby," I said. "Try to think of our beautiful hills and feel the strength they give you."

She handed me the baby. By the time we reached the roadway, we saw Joseph returning. Winded, he could hardly catch his breath.

"They are nice people," he said, "but there is no room. Many families are traveling to Jerusalem and returning from there."

Ezekiel said, "I will speak to him. He must have some room somewhere."

He turned the reins over to Joseph and ran ahead of us. We were close enough to see the inn ourselves. It looked old to me, as if it had lasted too many years and served too many people. Perhaps the wildness of the wind and sand gave it such a look. Another gust came up and blew sand into our faces. It blew hard against the trees, bending them to the ground.

Ezekiel returned to where we waited, half blown back by the wind. I said a little prayer to our God: "Protect us. Protect our Messiah. Do not let us stay outside in the cold and the wind."

Ezekiel caught his breath. "There is a stable. It's empty and clean. We'll be out of the wind and cold. This man is a good man. He said he would serve us food."

The innkeeper told us how sorry he was we could not stay in the inn. He showed us where we could wash, and we shared dinner with his guests. Mary could not eat. I felt her forehead, fearful she had a fever, but she did not show a temperature. She seemed weak and needed to rest. I coaxed her to eat some bean soup and helped her undress and crawl onto the warm pallet Joseph had made for her.

When she was comfortable, I handed her the baby, the little angel. He nursed hungrily. He had not cried on our journey until the wind began to blow, and then only a little bit. Occasionally he opened his blue eyes and stared at us. Ezekiel was entranced. "That's an old man," he said, grinning at the baby. Jeschu seemed to grin back. "I think he understands us all."

No one answered. We were tired. I didn't feel like joking about such a subject. A fear passed through me. What did we know about the conception of this strange baby, born without a father? He could be the devil pretending to be the Messiah. He could be the Messiah. He could be nothing but the product of a magician's lust. We didn't know.

I wish I could skip over what came next, as I do not approve of it. I am speaking of the three men who came to our barn to see Jeschu and what people made of it.

We had settled in for sleep when three men walked into the barn. They did not knock on the door. They opened it without saying a word. I felt prickles going through my body. These were no ordinary men but dressed in expensive velvet robes of red and blue and purple trimmed in gold. I had never seen such garments. I wondered if the innkeeper had sent them to share our stable. They were not dressed like Arabs or Hebrews or Romans, but like foreigners, perhaps merchants. Travelers often roamed through Judaea and Galilee from the East bringing fabrics of great value with them.

As they stood inside the door, a strong gust of love filled the room. I ignored it and wished they would go away or else tell us what they wanted. Did they want to stay in the stable with us or did they want to sell us goods? I was annoyed because it was late and they had not knocked.

"Are you going to leave here or do you want us to leave?" Joseph asked in a very friendly way.

The men stayed at the door, staring at the baby half hidden by Mary as he slept in her arms.

"We do not want fabrics," I said to them.

"These are not merchants," Ezekiel said.

Mary and the baby slept. Joseph sat in a corner far from the door. Ezekiel and I sat in the middle of the room. I could smell the grain and grasses stacked in a stall, a clean smell.

"We do not sell fabrics," one of the men answered. His face had a shine on it, and he was quite tall. "We have been told there is a newborn baby here, born with the mark of master upon his face, and we would like to look upon him."

"There is none such here," Ezekiel answered. "You must be mistaken. We are the only ones here, and you can see there is no newborn baby here."

Mary slept with a blanket covering her face; the baby was hidden in her arms. I wondered why Ezekiel did not acknowledge our baby, but then I realized he was afraid the strangers would take the baby away.

"We would not harm you," the stranger said, as if he knew what Ezekiel was thinking. "We have been guided by the night star and we come from Mesopotamia. That is some distance away, and we are weary. We would be very grateful if you would permit us to see the child and to give him our blessings and to take blessings from it, for we are told he is to be the Savior of the world, a great master."

"Who told you that?" Ezekiel wanted to know.

Joseph said not a word.

Another of the men, a short one, answered, "It has been foretold by an oracle and by the prophets: 'He shall come upon the earth unbidden and he shall live in sorrow, but he shall bring upon the world his spirit and his spirit will remain upon the earth while his body disintegrates, and with that disintegration he shall be known as Savior.' That is the prophecy."

Joseph spoke up. "We are weary travelers on our way to Jerusalem to be counted in the census. We do not have a messiah." He pointed to Mary. "That is my wife sleeping there."

His words seemed to dismiss the three men. I looked at Joseph, and then when I looked back at the three men, they had disappeared. "Did you see them go?" I asked Ezekiel.

"No, but I wasn't looking," he said. We were in our beds moments later ready for sleep. I remember nothing more of that evening. Our weariness was heavier than our puzzlement at the strangers.

"Can we put something against the door to keep us safe?" I asked my husband. Ezekiel got up from his pallet and said he would find something to put against the door. He saw a heavy rock and set it at an angle. Then he put our bundles against that. We fell fast asleep, being worn to the bone with our adventure and frightened at the changes we were undergoing.

Jeschu stayed asleep until morning, when Mary nursed and changed him. Joseph brought her warm water from the inn to wash him with. Now he was happy, and after we put on our outer garments, we took him outside with us. Mary went back to sleep for a little while longer.

The inn served an excellent breakfast with dried fish and cheeses, bread, and a hot drink of delicious herbs. We ate ravenously, so empty were we. Once revived, we felt ready to go on our way. But our daughter was not. I took her into the inn to a place where there was a washtub and soap, and we scrubbed her body with a cloth. She put on fresh clothes. Then she returned to her pallet. She was too weak to take care of herself. I thanked God many times for the privilege of taking this trip with her when I had exacted so many promises from God and Ezekiel that I would never leave Bethlehem.

I wished I could persuade Mary to return to our home, but she would not agree. She said she needed a day to rest and then she would be ready.

While Mary rested we met up again with the three men who had visited us in the stable and shared a conversation with them. When they came close, I could see the jewels sewn into their robes. I was overwhelmed. These were strange men of importance, foreign men. Their dark skin glistened with oil; they all had shining eyes that shot out light. The three of them asked for permission to come into the small room where we had been eating. It adjoined a large dining room filled with travelers. They bowed again as they walked in.

"We have come from Mesopotamia," one of the men said. "We are astrologers and we have followed the star Sirius because we were told it would lead us to the newborn Messiah."

I got up to leave and take Jeschu away from these men. How did they know that Jeschu had been born, that he was to be the Messiah? No one knew except the family and the rabbi and Joseph. None of us would ever tell anyone about it because we wanted to have our child grow up without any knowledge of his purpose on earth. When he grew up, he would know himself. I held Jeschu close to my breast, but he was visible. I got up to leave, but Ezekiel waved me down.

They said, "We saw the baby, and we know he is the Messiah. We have gifts for him. He is the true and real Messiah whom we have learned about in ancient times. He has come upon the earth to heal mankind of its fear of God and its fear of life and death. The Messiah will bring to the world a massive and great heart of love that he will leave upon the earth when his body is removed. That great heart of love will remain on earth in Jerusalem and bring anyone anywhere on earth comfort and healing, if only they ask for it in the Messiah's name."

"Joseph," I said, "Take the baby and let these men bless him as they have come to do."

Joseph took the sleeping baby into his arms, holding him as if he were more precious than a kingdom to a king. When they saw the child, the men in their beautiful robes bent their knees and bowed to the floor.

I clutched Ezekiel.

He said, "It must be true. We have given birth to our Messiah through the seed of our ancestors. Now we know it is true, and we are very humble that such a precious gift was bestowed upon us."

The men opened their bags of goods and took out cloth and incense and a heavy box. They put the things at our feet and said, "It is our wish that you receive these gifts for the Messiah and that you protect him with the gold we brought so that he will never suffer from poverty or want. We ask for nothing in return. We are blessed with the knowledge that you are going to protect this baby, and we will then live to see the Messiah."

The men vanished as if they were dissolved into the mist. No one saw them leave or tried to follow them. People concentrated on us. Some watched with curiosity because of the men's appearance. They saw the strangers give us a box, but they couldn't tell what it contained. From later developments, I realized they must have heard the word *Messiah*.

We hurried back into the stable. When we opened the box, we saw row upon row of gold shekels set like jewels, new and shiny, against the lining of purple velvet.

I gasped with shock. Ezekiel too seemed dazed. He picked one up, put it between his teeth, and then bit it. "It's real," he said, smiling.

We returned to our sleeping quarters to tell Mary our story. A soft smile illuminated her face. She did not seem surprised or elated.

"Aren't you excited?" I asked her. "Can you believe it?"

"People in the East are very close to God and can hear the talk of the angels," she said, sitting up and stretching her arms.

I smiled at her. "How would you know that, my daughter?"

She answered, "I just do."

"They probably are angels," Joseph agreed. "They came to protect the child from the evils of poverty and need."

I hid the coins by sewing them into the bottom hems of Mary's skirts and my own. "Each coin will cover a year of living, Ezekiel. Isn't that God's blessing?" Ezekiel nodded, but I could see he was uncomfortable about taking the money. I had wondered how we could stay in Jerusalem and live properly when none of us had enough money saved to take care of our needs. This was the most wonderful gift we could get because now we were not to worry about the cost of anything.

Even so, I was not convinced the baby was the Messiah, but I could not deny it. My mind would not accept the fact that such a miracle had come to pass in our family.

We prepared to leave the inn. A family—a man, a woman, and their two boys—claimed they had heard our conversation with the three foreigners.

"It is not possible," Ezekiel answered, angry. He stared at the couple, a short round woman with beady eyes like two black stones waiting to be discharged, and her man, a pale, unhappy person wearing a black, dusty robe. They were strangers to us.

"Where do you hail from?" Joseph wanted to know.

"Rakkath. We are going to Jerusalem," the man replied.

"Then go in peace. You will know the Messiah when he comes riding a donkey. Isn't that what Isaiah prophesied?"

The man shook his head, puzzled, and said, "That is so. Thank you, stranger. We will wait for the Messiah to come riding on his donkey, and then we will know he is the Messiah."

"Who were those strange men?" another man asked.

"They said your baby was the Messiah, didn't they? Why else would they bow to an infant?"

Joseph, as the father, said, "I never saw them before. They made a mistake. They insisted we take a gift, and we did. But we do not know them, and they thought we were somebody else. We must wait for the Messiah, and when he comes, we will know he is the Messiah."

We left the inn knowing that Jeschu would be talked about at the inn and from one end of Palestine to the other. We planned to deny everything. If the King of Jerusalem learned of the Messiah tale, we could expect trouble. He would destroy Jeschu, no doubt of that. He destroyed any-one who denied his power.

The King of the Hebrews, a secret organization, had in-sinuated its spies into all sects of Jews, Pharisees, Sadducees, the Essenes, the Zealots, and others, radicals who wanted to take back Jerusalem, their holy city, from the cruel Romans. None of us knew any more than that about the organization. It was spoken of in whispers that Herod, King of Jerusalem, used the men to spy on the Israelites. We were told in whis-pers that such men were taken away and destroyed without a trial. This meant that we must keep ourselves alert against the forces of evil that would certainly be active in the holy city.

I realized these three strangers were not strangers at all but deeply religious men. If they reported to the king, even telling him what he wanted to know—where the supposed Messiah, King of the Jews, was—they would be destroyed. They trav-eled a long distance to verify what they read in the stars.

"We should warn them," I suggested. "They have been watching for centuries for the Messiah of all men to appear, not just the Jews.

"The Messiah will bring all people of the world the same opportunity to live in peace and brotherhood through the energy they experience in their hearts," the men had told us. I re-called the strong aura of love in our room when those strangers walked into the stable. I was reassured that they were messengers from another world and not real people. They came to bring us the means to keep ourselves alive, not to be concerned for our future livelihood.

"We should have warned them of the danger to them," Ezekiel said. "But they left too fast. They just faded away like a dream."

As we gathered our belongings, our ears were still ringing with the anger of some of the people at the inn. They shouted their words, which were painful to listen to. "The Messiah! That little brat is the Messiah? They gave you gold. We saw them give you something. You made fools of those men, letting them bow to the ground before that sleeping baby."

Another one said, "That baby looks like an ordinary baby and not special. How dare you claim he is the Messiah so you can get money?"

Joseph seemed to enjoy watching these people get angry. He smiled and said, "This is my child, and we do not claim that he is the Messiah. We do not want anyone to believe he is the Messiah. He is so small. How can you tell? You can't and we can't."

A stream of people joined with us to journey to Jerusalem. Their stories and laughter shortened our time on the way, and we forgot our exhaustion climbing the hills.

Our journey took us from Bethlehem in Galilee on a winding hilly road through Samaria about two-thirds of the way, and then on to the route to Jerusalem.

As we neared the city, Joseph said, "My cousins, Zechariah and Elizabeth, live in Ain Karin. We are dirty and exhausted and need to rest before we find a place to stay in

Jerusalem. It will be crowded and unclean with so many people pouring in. My cousins will welcome us as guests.

"Elizabeth is expecting a baby," he added, "and she is well past forty. She will enjoy having company. From Zechariah we can learn if there is any talk in Jerusalem about the birth of a messiah. He is a priest in the temple."

Mary and Jeschu needed some time to recover, I thought. Ain Karim lay west of Jerusalem, a short way from the city, but restful and quiet, offering us peace in the hills.

My silent daughter spoke up to say, "Can we not do this, Father?"

Ezekiel looked at me. I could imagine what he saw. Our clothes covered in white sand, my face burned and brown from the sun, Mary with dark rings around her eyes from exhaustion. We had not tried to stay at another inn, thinking we would not find a room and that we could lie on the white stony grounds along the sides of the path. Also, we were afraid of attracting more attention to Jeschu.

Ezekiel gave us a beautiful smile. "There is nothing I would like more than to bathe and rest and not think of packing and unpacking."

We had sent no messenger to Joseph's cousins. I thought they knew we were coming, though, because Elizabeth and her husband waited in their gathering room, a long hall filled with plants and the perfume of roses. When they saw us walking toward their house, they came to meet us.

Zechariah kissed Joseph on his cheek, saying, "Welcome, my cousin."

Joseph said, "This is my wife and the baby, Jeschu, is my child." He turned to us, "And Mary's parents, Anna and Ezekiel."

I had never seen such a lavish house, for there was none such in our village in Galilee. I admired the furniture, handcrafted in fine wood, oriental carpets, luxurious copper pots holding the plants, and the sound of water dripping, cooling the hot, humid air.

Elizabeth took us away to the baths in the back of the house, and we luxuriated in them: water from the Dead Sea brought in hot and healing, then water from a nearby lake, clear crystal water. We washed our hair, Mary and I, while Elizabeth cooed over Jeschu, gently bathing him in a small tub made for the purpose.

The servants were told to prepare a meal for us: lamb; eggplant spiced and served with vinegar and boiled eggs; hot soup, the same my mother made, with vegetables and spices. Delicious cakes and sweets made of almonds ended the sumptuous meal, which made us forget our hardships and aches from the long trip. Mary rested while Elizabeth played with Jeschu, permitting him to exercise his arms and legs as he lay on a blanket on the floor. He cooed and slept and ate and slept, and Elizabeth cooed back with joy at the opportunity to be with the baby.

It's good practice," she said, smiling at me. "I can't wait to have this baby, such a blessing at my age. I thought we would never have a baby, but God is good and granted our prayers."

"You are not afraid?" I asked.

"No. I will live, and Jeschu will have a cousin."

Some five days later, Joseph suggested that we leave. "If you are rested," he said to me, "and if Mary is recovered." We left reluctantly because the visit had been so pleasant. Soon we saw the hills of Jerusalem. By the time we reached the city, Mary had recovered her energy and was fully healthy again.

CHAPTER IV

JERUSALEM

The first glimpse of Jerusalem sent my blood racing. It shimmered in the sun as if it wore a golden halo. Our promised land, the holy city of Saul and David and Solomon from the days of the biblical prophets, touched my soul. I wanted to kiss its earth.

"I can feel power from this land," I whispered to Ezekiel. "It grew from our blood." Ezekiel squeezed my hand to tell me he felt it, too.

Beyond our memory, Jerusalem has been called holy and prayers sent toward it. King Solomon did it honor, but God did it more. For Solomon's glory may fade, but the glory of Jerusalem's splendor will live as long as there is an earth. I do not know why. I only know that it is the heart of the earth and beats with its own tempo.

Jerusalem is God's promise to us, the same forever. Its narrow streets can never change. The hills will not change. The cobblestones will remain, as will the exquisite beauty of the dawn seen rising from the east in pale pink glory. In the quietness of its dark hours, when the stars illumine the heavens with a brilliant crown, I wonder whether Jerusalem itself is not a special star, to remain forever a promise.

We trudged tiredly into the city. It is not possible to climb the hills of Judaea without becoming weary to the bone. Tormenting thoughts like little bugs on the skin ran through my mind.

"Ezekiel," I said, as we rested in an empty field, "one more person knows about Jeschu."

He stopped me. "This is what we must say and believe. What else is there to say? Nothing happened. Joseph is the father of Jeschu. That is enough."

Ezekiel, normally so patient, answered me with irritation. I knew how tired he must be, weary with responsibility. But I had to say it.

"The man who did that act knows. He could have told those three travelers at the inn. He could have talked and spread rumors."

Ezekiel looked around, worried that someone was listening, but no one was near. "What are you saying?"

I tried to explain it better. "Those three men in Bethlehem, how could they have known about Jeschu? Why did they say he was the Messiah? That magician could have put Mary in a spell and told her she was going to be the mother of the Messiah. He could have held her in that spell, put the light on her, put her to sleep, and taken her. Then he could have gone around spreading a story that Mary's baby was the Messiah."

"Please, my dear one, please stop thinking," Ezekiel begged me. "Just stop it. If the rabbi doesn't know and I don't know, be satisfied that no one will know."

My voice rose. "We have to think, Ezekiel. This could

ruin Jeschu's life. Why should Mary give birth to the Messiah? She's an ordinary girl, even if we think she's an angel. She is special to us, but she isn't to other people. She's just a sweet, quiet girl. Now, those men told people our baby is the Messiah. What if Jeschu grows up believing he is? His life could be ruined, Mary's life, and ours, too."

Panic turned to terror in my heart. "I don't want my daughter to be the mother of the Messiah. Joseph's dream was only a dream. Those three foreign strangers could have been friends of the magician, who might have conspired with the devil about Jeschu's birth. That's why they brought the money."

Ezekiel looked at me hard. What could he say?

Our religion did not permit the use of magic or condone a belief in it. Our laws forbad us to consult magicians. Occasionally, in the village we saw the result of a woman who had been cursed, and then we would hear the story and shake our heads. To believe in magic was to become its victim, we were warned. We must never be afraid of it, but know that our Creator was our all, our one, the power within us and our healer.

So it could not be that a spell had been cast on Mary, who had no evil in her. Yet it worried me. Mary had no fear, no doubt. How could she be the victim of a magician? My common sense told me this was not possible, but my mother's heart was filled with fears. I was sure that if Jeschu were born of the magician, he would be evil and destructive. If he were born of God, with Mary as his mother, he was sure to be a messenger of his will.

Ezekiel came to me and cradled me in his arms. "Shush, my own soul, do not be afraid. If Jeschu is to be the Messiah, everything will be taken care of. If he is not, nothing will happen, and he will be known as Joseph's son. There is no reason to worry."

We asked a holy man in the town square if he knew where we could find rooms for about a week. He, too, was short and wore a long black beard with long hair, just like our own holy teacher. He told us we would find comfort and a welcome in the caves of the Essenes about a mile into the hills.

A young man greeted us when we reached the caves. "You are most welcome here," he said. This boy, Aram, said he was a student, an acolyte. His eyes shown bright as lamps and his sun-browned skin, so smooth and young, gave me a better balance in my belief of people, not all bad, not all good. I wondered, would this boy spend his life in darkness, in cells, dedicating himself to his Creator? Why did God create a beautiful world and loving people if he meant them to remain in a cave hidden from life, praising him? I could not find the sense in it and neither could Ezekiel.

The candle-lit passage brought us to a seemingly endless number of cells. Each provided space for a pallet to sleep on, with one corner given over to a fire for cooking. A table, two chairs, and a lamp completed the compartment. Ezekiel and I shared one room. Joseph and Mary and the baby had another. Joseph left Mary to stay in a room for ascetics who did not want to be with their wives for reasons of passion. Ezekiel and I were not allowed in there.

"What is it like?" I asked my son-in-law.

"Oh," he answered with one of his rare smiles, "it's the same as in our own caves where the men stay away from their wives and spend their time in prayer to Jehovah."

Later, on the street, some people from the inn passed by us. I recognized them and nodded. They were the ones who watched from a distance as the three strangers talked with us. They had seen Joseph take the box.

A heavy woman among them, disheveled black hair blowing into her face, yelled to passersby: "See the Messiah. A messiah has come. A baby. Come look at him." Her lips curled with a sneering smile. Then she cupped her fingers around her mouth and repeated the words again and again.

People passing glanced at us, then at her, and ignored her cries. A man who accompanied the woman tried to stop her shouting, but she persevered until we lost sight of her in the crowd and we no longer were her targets.

Joseph's eyes and set jaw told me he was angry even though he said nothing. This quiet man liked to work hard, eat his meals, have discussions on philosophy or religion with Ezekiel, and sometimes even with me. I did not know how to read Hebrew and had not studied beyond the stories Papa told. Still we shared our thoughts.

"What benefit do these people get from this?" Joseph wanted to know. "We are victims of lies and rumors. No one knows the truth. If some people called Jeschu the Messiah, they have no knowledge beyond rumor. They are evil.

"What have we got to do with that story?" he repeated in his bewilderment. "I never said the baby was the Messiah. Some strange men said it. I am merely the father. I wish to God they had never said anything. I wish to God we had never come to Jerusalem."

Members of one of the sects who lived in Jerusalem, the Sadducees, were fond of stoning anyone they thought had violated the law. Their method was very simple. They would wait until the person who was the object of their venom walked outside alone. Then the women, their aprons filled with stones, would rain them upon their victim. I envisioned my sweet, innocent daughter walking with her child to the square and suddenly being surrounded by those women, who would call her a liar and a fraud and stone her to death. That night I couldn't sleep.

"Ezekiel," I shook him awake. "Ezekiel, I can't sleep. I can't eat. They'll kill Mary if we stay here. I'm so afraid. I am going crazy with worry. Something keeps pushing me to get her out of the country, to get her away from Jerusalem and from Nazareth, far away where nobody will know about her."

Ezekiel tried to comfort me. "We will soon leave Jerusalem, my soul, and return to Bethlehem. We must go back and take care of our animals and land."

"We can't. We can't," I pleaded. "Just let me hide Mary and the baby in another country. She cannot stay in Palestine. She is in danger at home as well. Our child lives in a perfect world created from her experiences. She is not capable of coping with her baby, the jeers of people, the filth, the noise of the streets, and all the pandemonium rampant in Jerusalem."

Picture it as it was: the camels, mules, donkeys, and fowl ran about on the streets unrestrained, leaving their waste and foul odors. I did not like to walk there. No one seemed to care about disease, cleanliness, or purification, only that he went to the synagogue for his prayers. How foolish. How foolish.

I wondered if the magician—if indeed he were a magician—did not lay this curse upon us so that we would be haunted. Why? Why should a magician want to haunt us about the birth of a child? Was it not enough that he took Mary's body? Was it not enough that he fled so that we might never see and know him, or discover him, or lay claim on him? Had he not done enough?

A story spread in the caves, in its silent halls. A couple staying there, not Mary, claimed their child was the Messiah and must be hidden. They wanted to know, "Why do you claim your child is the Messiah?"

I did not answer because I did not know who was in truth and who had been deluded by a magician.

The woman, whose name was Rebecca, said, "Are you the people with the child who is to be the Messiah?"

Mary walked away with the baby. I said, "Why do you ask?"

Rebecca studied me for a long time. "I am told that I am to be the mother of the Messiah and that you are not the real grandmother of the Messiah."

I answered, "I do not claim to be the grandmother of the Messiah. I do not say my grandson is to be the Messiah or that your son is to be the Messiah. How can we know until it happens?"

Rebecca did not reply but walked away and did not speak to us anymore. Then she told my son-in-law that the King of the Jews, Herod, was going to have all the baby boys in Palestine killed to prevent a messiah from growing up and taking away his throne.

Joseph laughed when he heard this. "There is no such edict. Herod has said he would give the people of Jerusalem freedom to live any way they wanted to."

"But shouldn't we make sure? Can we find out whether what Rebecca said was true or wasn't?" I asked Joseph.

Joseph nodded. "I will do that. I will walk around the city and listen to the people and the Romans." Everywhere, Roman soldiers watched and stared.

That evening, when Joseph returned, we gathered in Mary's room. "The rumor is true. I heard one soldier tell another that Herod had given the order. He spoke Aramaic so I understood every word. We must leave these caves tonight because they will be searched."

Herod. Herod has learned that a messiah was born. That is what people whispered: "A search for Essene male infants by the Romans has begun. They must be destroyed in front of their mothers' eyes. Herod decreed it."

"Why? Why? Why does Herod care if the Israelites have a messiah?"

Joseph answered, "Because Herod is afraid that a messiah will become King of the Jews and take away his throne." Then he added, "Someone, an Israelite, it is said, has been searching the city for the baby Messiah to point him out to Herod. So now all boy babies born within the past two months must be destroyed because that man did not find him."

When we were in the caves in Jerusalem, I saw my father. He was old then and shrunken. His eyes sat deep in his head. He said to me, "I see you have a daughter of great beauty and also your own grandchild. How is it you have such a beautiful grandchild? Is it true that you are a good grandmother?"

I then brought Jeschu and Mary to him. "Bless the child," I told him. "He is your great-grandson." He stared at Jeschu and then said, "He has blue eyes. I think he will be the Messiah. Is that your belief, too?"

Mary smiled up at him. "He is just a little baby. But thank you for giving him your blessing." My father looked at Jeschu and Mary for a long time. They said nothing. Then he came to me.

"I am sorry," he said, "for what I did to you. You were difficult. I wanted you to be like your mother, but you would not. This is not the way I should have been, but now it is too late. I am an old man who will die soon, and you will have your grandson to live for. Now I see how much you are a person of great beauty and love. I wish I had been different because you would have loved me then, and we would have been close to each other.

"Please, forgive me. I am now learning many lessons. I wish I had never been a rabbi. I thought it was necessary to become the wisest rabbi in the world or the one with the most brains, and I did not want a daughter who would stand for her own self and be unafraid of me. Now I see that I was wrong. You were strong. I hope you will forgive me. I know now how important it is to be a human being who is kind and understanding and not bad-tempered. I regret my behavior with your mother. She was an angel, and she is to remain one in my memory. I pray that she has forgiven me. Now I must go."

I thought my father had lost his reason because I couldn't believe he would say these things to me, but I listened and I cried for myself and my mother, and then I felt how blessed I was to no longer be under the thumb of a man with such cruel ways with women even though he had changed. I reached up to him and said, "I forgive you, Father. But you must understand that I could never have been the daughter you wanted. I am still not able to be a good and obedient wife, but Ezekiel is very understanding and loves me as I am."

As we made our way out of the caves, we saw young mothers with infants lining the walls, waiting for permission to hide deep in the hidden caves, which were forbidden for anyone unpurified to enter. I prayed for them and their children. Mary wiped away a tear. Joseph, sad, and Ezekiel, angry, protected us on both sides. Jeschu remained invisible in his mother's robes.

CHAPTER V

ESCAPE

We thought we had found a safe place to hide, but no sooner had we moved our things than Joseph came back from the temple to say we must leave in a hurry.

"There are soldiers looking for us," he said, "because they have heard about the men who came to the inn and gave us money. They want the money, and they want to kill the baby. We must hurry this very day to go into another country so that Jeschu cannot be found."

Mary did not become in the least perturbed. She said, "Nothing can happen to my baby because he is under the protection of God himself."

"Mary," I said, "no matter how much protection we give this angel, it is still a living baby and can be destroyed."

Ezekiel agreed and started tying up our bundles of clothing and loading them on the mules and the donkey. "We must go right now," he said. "We must leave before the day is ended."

Our supplies once again on the donkey and mules, we made our way to the outskirts of Jerusalem, walking slowly so as not to attract attention. I thought I heard Jeschu give a strong yell, as if he wanted to talk to us about our problem.

"That is your imagination," Ezekiel told me as I walked by his side. He laughed. I laughed too. My depression and fear lifted momentarily. Joseph walked with Mary and we held onto the animals.

My grandson slept peaceably, not aware of the great stir his birth had caused. We hid him well, next to Mary's breast, under a wide cloak, nowhere visible. Mary looked too much the child to be questioned.

We came onto the main thoroughfare. Soldiers stood lined along the road to search travelers for concealed weapons, smuggled food, clothes, or jewels. And now they wanted to find the Messiah.

"Be calm, be calm," Ezekiel whispered. If we hurried or paid attention to them, they would stop us. People gathered together to pass the soldiers as a group. The soldiers sometimes pulled one person from the cluster to search, but did not bother with them usually. We joined a crowd, lagging a little behind. The road from Jerusalem to Bethlehem and south to Hebron made a well-traveled pathway until we turned off the main path toward the Great Sea, toward Gaza. I didn't know where we were going because I couldn't figure it out. Ezekiel said we were walking south along the border of Judaea.

"Alexandria," Joseph told me. "We are going to Alexandria in Egypt, where we can live and not be talked about as parents of the Messiah."

We stopped for the night outside of Jerusalem, too weary to move another step. Ezekiel scouted for an empty field as the sky darkened. He found one past an incline toward a hill where he thought we would be safe from intruders. Mary took some soup with bread and fell asleep nursing the baby. In the morning we washed in water by the field, ate our cheese and dried fish with bread and cold tea, and then proceeded on our journey.

The countryside changed. Sand and wind and more heat were our constant companions. We also felt as if we did not know our people any longer, although we were still in Judaea. Dark of skin, with enormous eyes and very silent, Egyptians or Palestinians moved with us, dressed like us except many wore turbans on their head to keep out the heat of the sun.

Eventually we reached a little village. Stalls filled with foods, clothes, and household items lined the street. We were all feeling dazed and ready to give up, so our spirits lifted when we saw the stalls. Ezekiel examined the fruit at one stand.

"It is fresh from the harvest," he pronounced. We bought a large amount of figs, grapes, and dates, all sweet and fresh, and we moved into a field near the village to enjoy the feast.

Heat burned into our bodies, leaving us lethargic. Finally our little caravan moved on. When we came to another village, Joseph asked if there was any place to stay. "We do not have an inn," the man said, "but there is someone here who likes to welcome travelers and visit with them."

We followed his directions to find this person's house. "Welcome to Adora, our village of the Great Tree, and come into my house where you can refresh yourselves," a handsome, elderly man, all smiles, said in greeting when we came to the house. "My name is Amon."

This kind man asked no questions. He told us we would be on the road for a number of days before we reached Gaza, that we must change our clothing for lighter ones and find more ways to make our trip simpler. Our bundles took up too much space and required great effort in packing and unpacking. If we needed more food, we could find it in villages along the coast. We did not have to worry about our safety in Egypt because the Egyptians were not afraid of strangers and did not want to harm them.

Our host offered us a hot meal of lamb and sauce with grains, and more fruit and nuts. We relaxed with food and laughter until we forgot how tired we were and how much we wanted to rest. "Behind my house there is another, where you may wish to spend the night," Amon said. "You will find water at the well and you will find rest."

"You are a very kind man," Ezekiel said. "We bless you for your goodness." Joseph asked Amon if he knew of a rabbi in Alexandria who could give us some help in finding a place and getting acquainted with people and the city.

"I can help you," Amon said. He went into his house and brought out a scroll to write a message on. "This rabbi is a friend. He will help you."

CHAPTER VI

A NEW LIFE BEGINS

"What a world we live in," I said to my husband, trying to be cheerful. "There is so much beauty I wonder that we ever do anything but stare at it." We looked a sorry group as we made our way onward once more. Our feet slid in the sand, and we had to grope for a solid place to step. The sun had already begun to burn us, and we were just beginning our journey to the sea. We plodded on, our feet crunching the sand over the distance to Alexandria.

"Can we take a boat when we reach the sea?" Mary asked. "We have the money. It is such a long walk for the animals and for you, Mother."

"For all of us," Ezekiel said.

Our tiny baby Messiah cried occasionally as he suffered from heat, sand, and wind. We kept cold cloths on his body and head, constantly changing them, but the heat had become a devil intent on devouring us.

The sun burned through our clothes with no pity even though it was late autumn. My eyes became twin flames. In spite of coverings and shades, I could no longer endure the blaze consuming my back. Mary's face reddened until I worried she would become unconscious from the burning of the sun. There was nothing for us to do but continue, for we were in empty space except for the path taking us toward Gaza and the sea.

Thoughts on the origin of my grandson swirled through my head in hysterical fashion, round and round. The baby is not yet two months old. Anyone can see he is an ordinary baby, like any other infant. How could he be sent from God to teach us better ways? There is no mark on him to say he is to be a holy man. But there was the money to think about. Why would men give us a fortune to protect an ordinary baby? How could my daughter have been impregnated without a man? Or was there a man? My thoughts whirled around and around.

"Drink water. The heat eats us up," Ezekiel reminded us again and again. We drank and drank until we ran out of water. I panted for breath.

Ezekiel was worried. "Let us stop and rest," he said. "Let's put up the tent." Sweat ran down his face like water. He must be suffering as much as I, my heart's soul. He gave me a tender look, a most caring one. I wanted to burst into tears. We still had hours to burn until the night came, for we could see the sun blazing at us just slightly below its high point. Would we all die in this waste of nothingness? In reality, it seemed so. But Mary's serenity never wavered. I heard her words in my ears. "You are safe. It is written, Mother."

Joseph shouted, "Look!" We turned to where he pointed. In the distance blue water danced in the sunlight. "It's the Great Sea!"

We wanted to run to reach the cool water and bathe our faces in it. None of us could. We dragged ourselves there at the point of collapse and fell upon a shore of wet sand. My senses swam. I felt faint and at a far distance from what was happening. A man hurried to us with a flagon of water. Another man brought a flagon to Mary. Someone poured water over my face to revive me. Mary lay on the sand in a faint. A woman bathed her head and neck. Joseph disappeared into a bathhouse, and after the animals were given water and put to rest, Ezekiel followed him.

The baby lay naked in a boatlike pan, bathed in cool water. One woman, her head covered, her robe black, came with fruit and asked us in a friendly manner where we were going. Were we taking the boat? We nodded yes. "It will be here soon, if you want to go to Alexandria."

We revived ourselves and found a place to bathe while we waited for our boat. Men pushing little carts of food came to us offering a variety of vegetables and fruit, eggplant prepared in different ways, apricots, almonds, spiced delicacies, much the same as we had at home. As we cooled off, our appetites returned.

I watched the harbor water dipping and dancing with boats of all kinds, their white sails fluttering against the skyline and the blue water.

"Oh," Mary gasped. "It is so lovely. How blessed we are to see this."

Once we located shelter and space on the boat, Ezekiel sang songs as his thanksgiving for a safe journey. Mary joined him. They sang one after another into the scarlet sunset until the last rays were gone. People stared at us, puzzled at the songs and at us. We smiled back at them, waving our hands with affection.

Ezekiel put the choice to me. "Will you want to stay in Alexandria, or do you want to return to Bethlehem?"

"Perhaps with a year's rest, I will be able to return," I replied. "By then, my feet should be healed and my head clear enough to walk back." We smiled at my joke.

"Alexandria is famous for its libraries," Joseph said. "It is a great center for learning. Many distinguished scientists and teachers live there. One of them is named Andronicus. I would like to know him."

Andronicus, though old, would play a role in Jeschu's education, but for now the baby rested, with never a thought of what his future was going to be.

We arrived in Alexandria after two more days of sailing. What a picturesque city, not in the way Jerusalem is beautiful, but in the strength of its colors, white buildings, white sands, blue sea, and waves of people wearing brilliant shades of purple, red, blues, and greens.

Ezekiel brought the note from our Great Tree friend to Rabbi Salek.

"Your friend is a good man," the holy man said. "What kind of work are you looking for?" His eyes turned to Joseph.

"I am a carpenter," my son-in-law answered.

"There's plenty of work for a good carpenter," the rabbi responded. "I know just the neighborhood. You will have Essene neighbors. I see you are Essene."

I wondered how he could see this because we had told him nothing, but these holy men seem to have insight into us and know about us without being told anything.

Rabbi Salek would be our friend. Like other rabbis he was short with a long black beard, but his warm eyes glowed with mischief, humor, and common sense.

He took us on winding streets and down little pathways. My feet were swollen and the discomfort caused little moans to escape from me. But people pulling carts and wagons loaded with merchandise fascinated me, and I forgot the pain. It seemed as if we walked for miles. I was ready to collapse, but then we made a turn and came upon what looked like a bazaar of little shops, one lined next to the other, selling carpets, pottery, cloth, pillows, fruit and vegetables, clothing, household supplies, implements, and anything else you could ask for.

"I know of a house near here enclosed in a court so that you have room for your goat and your other animals as well as yourselves," Rabbi Salek said, leading the way to it.

He took us past the shops and the clatter of hooves on the hard rock street, around the edge of the street, and there showed us the house. The street noise stopped. There was no more clatter. I thought it perfect even though I had not seen the inside.

"Thank you, Rabbi," Joseph said, pressing a silver denarius into his hand.

The rabbi pretended not to notice. He nodded goodbye, turned, and left. He paused and then turned around again.

"You will be happy here if you stay out of the way of the Egyptians. Most of them are willing to let Israelites live here, but there are others who would like to kill us and will kill us if we are in their way. The house is open. I will arrange for the man who owns it to come by for the money."

Mary's energy came back. The baby cooed and cooed in relief, I thought. Ezekiel took care of the animals. "We will not need them here," he said. "Only the goat, for milk and cheese."

We found the house remarkably clean and very light.

"Surely we have angels watching over us," Mary insisted, "or else how could we have found this lovely house waiting for us? It is welcoming us. Can't you feel it?" She put the baby down on a pallet of straw brought along.

We examined the place room by room and exclaimed our pleasure at finding three separate small rooms and a general open space for sharing food and companionship in community living. The enclosed outside court had borders of flowers: hyacinths, lilies, and lovely lilac. I wondered how they would survive when our goat was set free.

"We'll build a pen for him," Ezekiel promised me.

Joseph and Ezekiel went shopping for furniture. They bought a table and chairs and a robe holder for our clothes, beds to sleep on, a cradle for the baby, a bench for the community room, colorful pillows of leather and velvet, and tallow lamps for lighting.

Mary took one room for herself and Jeschu. We took another, and Joseph had the last. We rejoiced because we had privacy, more than we had ever known.

After we settled down, Ezekiel and I explored Alexandria's strange, very old buildings, large and white. I could not tell what they were.

"That one is more than three hundred years old," Ezekiel said in wonder. "It contains the most famous library in the world. It's the one Joseph told us about, remember?"

I said I wanted to go inside and look.

Ezekiel went up to the doors, and knocked. A dark-skinned Egyptian opened the door and invited him in. My husband came out a few minutes later, awe in his eyes.

"It is a school of philosophy and a museum. There are rooms and rooms of ancient scrolls in Hebrew, Greek, Latin, and languages we don't even know. I asked for permission to bring you in, but they said women are not allowed."

Why couldn't I see the library and the museum? Ezekiel taught me to read Aramaic early in our marriage, although women were not permitted to learn. Such a gift might give them power, it was thought.

I said to Ezekiel, "I will talk to them."

Ezekiel brought me to the door. The same man answered.

"This is my wife. She wants to see the library and the museum. Is she not permitted to even look at it?"

The man stared at me as if he knew me. Somewhere I knew him, too. Of course, that was impossible. He bowed to us to come in together. Ezekiel went to an open scroll to read it. I marveled at the architecture and pieces of antiquity, weapons, tools, carvings, exquisite inlaid jewelry, and glazed pottery in the museum, the only museum I had ever seen. It was an experience I would treasure for my lifetime. The Egyptian came to us when we were ready to leave. He escorted us to the door, staring at me as if he was puzzled, but he said nothing.

I asked Ezekiel what he thought was wrong with women that they were not permitted to learn or work or teach, only to stay in the house and bring up their children without guidance.

Ezekiel said we were not created to do work outside the house, where men could get at us and use us for their needs.

That is why we had to live such hidden lives. We could not defend ourselves against men.

I told my husband that we were able to take care of ourselves if we had to. It was not fair to bind us.

"You, Anna, could take care of yourself because you are free," Ezekiel acknowledged, "but other women are brought up to fear the world. They could not protect themselves."

A strong anti-Hebraic feeling developed soon after we arrived. Saloma, a Hebrew neighbor, tried to explain it to me.

"It's always the same," she said. "These people worship many gods. They wonder why we don't. We say we believe in one God, Jehovah. They take it as an insult to them, their gods, and their country. They want us to acknowledge the power of Omnipater, their god, by bowing to him when we see his statue. Now they say we cheat them when they buy from us."

I tried to explain my beliefs to Saloma. "The confusion comes from not understanding that all things arise from one. There is only one Creator, one God. This Creator opens its seed and spreads them over the world. The world cannot control the spreading of these seeds; they fly like bees to a flower and they spread everywhere. Whoever takes in the seed takes on the godlike traits of their Creator. They believe they are God. How can there be more than one Creator when we are all the same in heart and body and only look different?

"When we change ourselves into people of God and not God-worshiping people, by knowing the seed of God is in all of us, then we will be brothers and sisters free of intolerance. We will know who we are."

"I don't understand," Saloma said, staring at me as if I were speaking madness.

I had no more explanation. She left, and we decided to stay in Alexandria and make it our home, at least until Herod was removed as king. Ezekiel planted herbs, a pomegranate tree, and grapevines over the walls.

"Let's put in a fig tree," I begged. "It will remain here forever."

Mary developed into a healthy young woman, still very quiet, almost as silent as Joseph. Thoughts of danger to Jeschu left us. No one was looking for a little messiah.

CHAPTER VII

THE BOY JESCHU

Jeschu's growing years passed quickly. We watched him change from infant to baby to little boy to budding scholar all too soon. Sometimes the boy teased his mother or me. Still, the child mostly stayed quiet and thoughtful, as Mary and Joseph did. "The little Messiah," as Joseph referred to him, never dreamed he had been born to teach the world a new way of living. I no longer dwelled on Jeschu's strange birth.

We gave him freedom to think and talk. He asked endless questions.

"Mama, what is the size of the moon? Why don't we eat pork? What is your name in Arabic?" He learned Arabic, but we spoke Aramaic as our families had. Jeschu spoke both Arabic and Aramaic. "Show me where Bethlehem is. Why don't we go back there?"

He learned Greek and Latin. He also read Hebrew, as his father taught him his letters, and he knew how to read the word combinations as if he knew them before.

"He'll soon be as tall as a beanstalk," Ezekiel said one morning when Jeschu left the house.

"Yes," I answered. "He is growing faster than normal and so is his mind. He's only seven and talks like an old man of wisdom. Jeschu could pass for thirteen, being so tall and so full of knowledge."

Joseph took him to Andronicus, the astronomer and philosopher and scientist, who put him in a school of mystery. Jeschu spent each week with Andronicus, leaving Monday morning and not coming home until Friday in time for the Sabbath rituals. One time, without telling anyone in the family, I hid my face in my cloak and followed Jeschu and his father as they went to the school. They walked to a strange temple surrounded with walls. Joseph opened a gate and disappeared with Jeschu. But I could see nothing, hear nothing, do nothing. I had no idea what they did.

One thing I am sure of is that Jeschu learned from the school how to create whatever he wanted out of the air. A number of teachers could also do this, Jeschu said.

He memorized chants and liked to sit in the courtyard at home to practice them. When our magician chanted, dark blue and purple lights danced in front of my eyes.

What is to become of my grandson? I asked myself. I thought about it and then spoke to Ezekiel. "Mary and Joseph do not listen to me. They live in dreams of their own and pay no attention to my warnings. Is it not tampering with God's commands when they send their son to an Egyptian for learning? Where has it ever been written or spoken that a Hebrew should learn the magic ways of Egyptians? The

Hebrews are of Judaea and not of Egypt. They have their own disciplines and ways of praying, not like the Egyptians.

"Jeschu will not be a good Israelite or a rabbi. He is learning too many strange things and thinking in a different way from us, practicing heathen traditions."

My husband had no answer. He shrugged his shoulders and shook his head. Jeschu did not give me any help, either. The boy didn't listen to what I said, and I couldn't understand what he said. The child talked about the stars as if they lived here on the planet with us.

Jeschu would answer, "They do. They do, Grandmother. They share the same world we live in, and we are part of them."

He lived in wonder at the mysteries he learned about in Andronicus' school.

"I can hear the voices of the people no longer on the earth when I listen to the air," Jeschu said. "Try it, Grandmother. Just listen to the air. You will hear."

"Anyone as different as my grandson may get his rewards in heaven, but he will not get them when we return to Palestine," I told Ezekiel. "He is courting death with his way of talking, for he will be branded a devil. In Palestine he will be stoned, beaten, or whipped to death for blasphemy."

Ezekiel also wanted the boy taken away from the Egyptian, but his answer was measured. "I have no right to question Joseph's decisions for Jeschu. Joseph is a great scholar and thinker. He sees this work as part of Jeschu's education, necessary for the future," Ezekiel said.

"But is Joseph the only one who can choose what is good for Jeschu? A mother has no right to speak to her husband about such things? A grandmother has no right at all to speak? This is wrong. We are his blood relatives," I argued.

Joseph did not get angry with me when I asked such questions, but he did not answer me either. I did not understand Jeschu. Every night I prayed to God to make him normal, not special. It is a curse to be different. I worried that he might leave his people and become an idol worshiper, or that he might forget all he had learned when he was put into the hidden school of the Essenes. I would have given my heart to God without question if I thought that would change my grandson into a normal, healthy little boy.

"Why do you not put Jeschu in school with a rabbi?" I asked Joseph. I stared at him, piercing him with accusatory looks. He knew how much I disapproved of what he was doing. Jeschu stood by silent and still. His eyes were so big and so blue, I wanted to dye them black like ours. But I could not change the color of his eyes. It was not so rare. Mary's eyes were blue and sometimes a strain of blue eyes appeared among us. But that it should happen to two in my family made me unhappy. It stirred up fears. What really happened to my daughter years ago? She was never the same. Mary lived with us and did her duties as she should. But she also lived in another world, a world of fantasy and dreams.

Joseph sometimes tried to explain his plan. "It is best for the boy to understand more," he would say.

"To understand about stars and figures and laws?" I asked him. "What about the scriptures and the laws of God given to us by Moses? What about Daniel? His faith in God permitted more miracles to happen than any Egyptian ever performed."

I knew what I needed to know, but my grandson Jeschu knew more than he needed to know. Jeschu said he would like to walk to the ends of the earth and see for himself where that was and what happened to people when they got there. What kind of talk is that for a child seven years old? He spoke of Ra, the sun god, of Thoth, and of stranger names I cannot remember. The boy learned the history of Egypt.

"Jeschu," I asked. "Do you remember everything you are ever told? You have a parchment scroll inside you, and it never stops unwinding."

Jeschu looked at me sideways with a grin on his face. "Grandma, I'm hungry. Do we have something I can eat now?"

Grandmothers are for serving food, not thinking, my grandson was telling me. Women are not interested in stars and gods. Joseph was. Jeschu was. Ezekiel pretended not to be interested, but I saw him watching Joseph teach Jeschu.

Ezekiel explained to me that Joseph was a deep scholar and knew about stars. He and Jeschu sat under the night sky and identified the faraway objects night after night.

"Teach him to be a carpenter," I said to Joseph. "He's going to need to know how to do that. Take him with you to your work and let him learn your trade."

Joseph nodded in agreement. "In time, little Grandmother. When Jeschu is ready."

Sometimes I forgot that Joseph was an Essene and brought up with as much knowledge as a rabbi, so that the Hebrew lessons he gave Jeschu prepared him for his bar mitzvah.

When Jeschu was a few years older, he learned how to heal illness and deformities, using his hands to send the sick ones energy. He raised bodies of the dead through his breath, chants, and the use of those energy lights.

I did not know how I learned of this, and I couldn't endure not to know. Perhaps Ezekiel spoke with Joseph and then told me.

The teachings given to my grandson were lessons meant to be used for healing people. Jeschu learned secrets not given to many to know, secrets never revealed to those outside of a certain brotherhood. The masters knew how to breathe life into a corpse. They performed surgery through hypnosis with their concentrated willpower, never cutting the body.

These masters taught only those brought to them through the guidance of mentors who walked the path of light in all countries. They sent their disciples to Alexandria and the secret Temple of Mysteries. None else could be initiated.

This I did not know then but found out much later in a talk with Jeschu, who verified with a nod of his head the conclusions I had made about the Temple of Mysteries.

It was to my wonder that Jeschu received permission, as a concession to the Master Andronicus, to leave the temple. His oath was one of silence for his lifetime: he would never reveal his attendance or what he learned there. But I would clear up the mystery that confounds the world as to where Jeschu was taught.

Are such mysteries as Jeschu wrought possible for others to perform? I would answer yes, of course. They are not only possible, they are also natural. What Jeschu could do so easily, anyone with the power of divine faith, which is true love, can accomplish as seeming miracles.

Jeschu, in the summer when he did not attend the Temple School of Mysteries, was a different child. He dutifully continued his Hebraic teachings with Joseph and his grandfather in preparation for his bar mitzvah, attended the synagogue, and also worked as an apprentice to his father as a carpenter.

"Isn't it about time," I asked, smiling at my son-in-law, "that we enroll Jeschu in a school of the Essenes and let a rabbi teach him our laws?"

Joseph said, "I will take him away, Mother, when I am told to take him away, and not sooner."

Ezekiel wanted Jeschu to leave the Temple of Mysteries, but he would not go against Joseph and Mary's plans. He worried because it was long past the time that Jeschu should be placed in the Essene School of the Caves in the islands, not too far from where we were living, if he were to receive studies for his bar mitzvah.

"We are planning to move to the caves when Jeschu turns thirteen," Joseph said. "I will prepare him for his bar mitzvah, and it will take place on his thirteenth birthday."

"I do not want to live there," I told Ezekiel. "Can we not stay here in Alexandria? We would still be close to Mary, Joseph, and Jeschu? Need we go to live among the Essenes? They are so strict. I will be separated from you, for men and women do not live together. You know that. We would only be able to visit each other."

"I know," my husband said. "Would you like to return to Bethlehem instead of staying in Alexandria? We could go there by boat. It would not be the terrible trip we made to get here so long ago."

Ezekiel's beautiful black hair had turned almost gray. I, too, saw gray hair weaving through my own. Lines in our faces told us we were living our autumn years, a time for peace and pleasure in the fruit of the tree of life. Soon we would be gone, for a lifespan was little more than forty years and we had passed that, and Joseph had as well. It was possible that Mary would face the future with Jeschu alone.

"Let us stay here in Alexandria until we learn what Joseph decides to do," I answered Ezekiel. "Then, if we can, let us return to our home of bliss."

Ezekiel grinned and grabbed me in his arms. "Bliss is right here, now, my own soul's being."

When Jeschu turned thirteen, he had his bar mitzvah. Joseph arranged for it to take place in the Essene caves near Dumyat to the west of where the Nile River flows into the sea. We went by boat on the Great Sea to attend his bar mitzvah ceremony. Jeschu, Joseph told us, would read from the Torah and give a talk.

We enjoyed being on the water once again after walking on land for so long a time. The water rocked us in a rhythm so that we were lulled into a song the sea sings, a lullaby. It gave me a feeling of being safe and protected from the harshness of the earth.

We were greeted by a small group of men and women who lived separately in the dark rooms in a cave. They made a cave where there was no cave, deep and dark in the earth. I did not like it. But the rooms were very large. I suppose they built the cave to be safe from attack because they could not be seen from the outside.

Jeschu took the most devout vows of celibacy and vows of fasting and self-denial. He could wear no clothes except a loin-cloth and a robe. This Essene sect taught that the Essenes were a higher order of men through discipline of the mind and em-powering of the will to serve God. The Essenes stressed truth, discipline, and obedience. They did not lie, cheat, or pretend. Jeschu would learn to resign himself to abstinence and the dis-covery of what truth was according to the Essenes.

Jeschu's other life, his education at the Temple of Mystery and its secret teachings, were not spoken of, just as the story of his mysterious birth and mission were subjects sealed on our lips. We well knew that he could be excommunicated for delv-ing into mysteries not of the scriptures. We were ordered not to study or read anything unless it was prescribed by our rabbi.

I did not break that law. Ezekiel did not break that law. But Mary and Joseph did. Their silence was a lie they chose to keep. They knew it, and they kept silent. We would not say anything. Jeschu said nothing. He was not asked if he had studied other teachings, and he did not say.

He came before us and recited his readings perfectly. He spoke in Hebrew. He spoke simply and wisely. Jeschu spoke of man and man's duty to himself. God had given all men the com-mandment that they shall not worship other gods before him.

The rabbis nodded their heads in agreement and approval. I, too, know that God dwells in flowers and trees. God is in the rivers and lakes. God created this world. But what is this world without life breathed into it? God created man. But what is man without breath? God created himself in us through our breath; it is life we breathe in and out, Jeschu told us.

Those listening thought Jeschu gave a very good talk.
Now in the quiet, night covered us. The stars, clustered thick
overhead, spread a bright light when we went outside to sit
in the dark. We sang and chanted while the nearby water
lapped around us.

There was not too much celebration, for the Essenes did
not dance or play instruments. But we ate food and talked.
That is a wonder, for often the Essenes did not consider food
important. Some bit of cheese or vegetable was all they put
upon the table. This time there was plenty of fruit and wine.

We returned to Alexandria to live while Jeschu and Mary
and Joseph stayed with the Essenes. I felt better going back
to Alexandria. If Mary and Joseph decided to leave the caves,
they would have our place to come to. I could not believe
they would stay long in that place.

I could not see what Jeschu was doing, but I knew of the
austerity, the prayers, the morning rituals, the prayers for the
dead, and the prayers for the living. I knew of the chants. I
knew of the long days of fasting, the study of the scriptures
and the long hours of discussion that took place. I knew of
those things although I never participated. I knew what was
happening there, and I waited for the day when Mary and
Joseph would return.

CHAPTER VIII

RETURN TO ALEXANDRIA

M ary, Joseph, and Jeschu returned to Alexandria after a ritual was performed proclaiming Jeschu a holy man on his sixteenth birthday. The boy left Alexandria a child of thirteen and returned to the city a man of sixteen. I stared at him, unbelieving.

"You've grown another foot," I told him. "You're as tall as your father." I'd forgotten how deep blue his eyes were. They blazed lights. His skin, firm and pale, glistened. The boy-man was nobody I knew. I had to learn who this person was. Ezekiel agreed. I could see his pride in his grandson, a rabbi at sixteen, but we needed time to get used to his new state.

"Tell me, Grandson, did you finish your work? Are you a holy man?"

Jeschu laughed. "Grandmother, I missed you very much. I missed your caring about me and feeding me and watching me. Yes, it is very good to be back here with you and Grandfather." He embraced Ezekiel and me.

"But, Jeschu, tell me. Are you a holy man now? Did you learn the Hebrew traditions? Have you accepted them?"

Jeschu seemed to struggle for the right words to prepare me.

"Grandmother, I read the ancient scriptures and gave my interpretation of their meaning when I could. My master ordained me. He laid his hands on me and conferred a part of the spirit of Moses on me just as Moses did to Eleazar, the son of his brother Aaron, and gave me instructions."

"What does this mean, Jeschu? Can you be a teacher in Galilee? Will you return there with us when we leave? We plan to go back to Bethlehem."

"My covenant is with God, Grandmother. How I work, earn my bread, or where I go to perform my work is not directed by the Essenes or anyone. I am told to choose my destiny as I will it."

We kept our goat tied to a post. She no longer gave milk, but we had grown so fond of her that we considered her part of the family and would not let her go. Jeschu came up to her and caressed her. She seemed to recognize him and gave him a nuzzle of happiness. Jeschu slept in the courtyard, as the weather was warm and it was pleasant there, even though he had to share his space with our goat.

I had prepared a feast of cheeses, fruits, and vegetables, but not of meat. I supposed the family had returned to the Essene tradition of not eating meat, but that was not true. They had been looking forward to eating their favorite roast lamb. Even Jeschu did not plan to continue observing the Essene traditions concerning food.

Mary talked to us about life in the caves. Joseph gave me the warmth of his smile, while Mary hugged me. "It's so good to be back here, Mother. I'm so glad to be back."

We had seen each other on two brief occasions when Ezekiel and I went to the cave to visit, but I was never alone with her to find out what she was feeling and what was happening. With her words, I knew that she too found living in caves a hardship, although she would not tell me so directly.

"What did you do?" I wanted to know. "How did you spend your time?"

Mary smiled softly. She was so beautiful I just wanted to stare at her face and listen to her voice, soft and musical. "There was plenty to do," she said. "We had our morning prayers, our household work, carding and weaving. Then we had an hour of silent prayer. We were not permitted to be together on the Sabbath. That was when everyone spent the day praying, but we could be together the next day. Jeschu, Joseph, and I enjoyed those times." Mary paused and remembered again. "That was the day I really enjoyed. It was a miracle to see the way Jeschu grew and changed into a man. Even a week made a change."

Jeschu decided he wanted to be a carpenter like his father and not a rabbi. The family was gathered in our sitting room when he made this announcement. No one spoke. I sat in a reverie, thinking we had been living in this same house in Alexandria since Jeschu was a baby. It seemed we were just the same as when we came, as if we had been waiting all this time for Jeschu to grow up so that we could protect him from whatever his destiny was. Now his plan was to be a carpenter.

Ezekiel and I both wondered how he was going to be satisfied working as a carpenter when he had all that knowledge in his head. He was not a carpenter. He would not be content putting pegs into their place, or placing stones where they belong, or building and repairing. What kind of a task was that for a boy who was already a rabbi?

Joseph encouraged his son and often talked with him about subjects he studied. Yet he did not seem to question the choice Jeschu had made. He said Jeschu must walk with his own steps in his own way.

Mary would never interfere with a decision Joseph or Jeschu made. She was always like this. I think she was a happy woman. Mary had lost the personality she had as a girl, when she was so interested in people, animals, and helping others. Now she was waiting, waiting, and waiting, while Joseph went out and worked.

Jeschu accompanied his father to his work as if he knew nothing else but that he was to be a carpenter. What about the miracles he performed with a wave of his hands? What about all his teachings? Why did he not call himself a rabbi? Instead, like any other workman, he left with his lunch and came back tired at the end of the day. He did not make any friends. At night he studied.

I saw myself succumbing to the aging process, the hair at my temples turning gray, my body softening and widening. Ezekiel's hair, too, was becoming salt-and-pepper gray. He had developed a curve to his shoulders and a bend to his head.

Mary and Joseph still seemed very young to me, although Joseph was much older than Mary, who looked like a child. Her figure remained the same, not changed from that of a sixteen-year-old girl. Joseph, too, appeared to be the same.

But Jeschu, how clearly I see him. He was tall for our people, about five feet ten inches, very slender, his beard bushy and black, his face a perfect oval with broad cheeks and high forehead, a perfectly shaped nose and those very blue eyes.

His hair, black and curly, hung to his shoulders. In many ways he resembled Mary. She too had a perfect oval face. There was sweetness in that face. I suppose by not ever worrying or thinking about what might happen or could happen or did happen, she avoided that feeling of pressure that makes lines and aging.

I wanted to go back to Bethlehem. "I am ready now if you want to leave," Ezekiel said.

"Do you think our house is still there? Will my carpets still be on the floor? Surely no one would dare to use it," I mused to myself, but loudly enough for Ezekiel to hear me.

"The house is still there. What could happen to it? But we will have work to do when we get back." The animals, I knew, would have disappeared or died. They were left in the care of Joseph's sons, who would be men now. But the land and the house should still be there.

I thought of it with longing. I thought of the hills, the quietness, and the friendliness of the neighbors who knew us.

Ezekiel looked at Joseph and Mary as they walked into the room. "Anna and I will be returning to Bethlehem. Will you join us?"

"We cannot go," Joseph answered. "But you can. We cannot leave yet."

"Why not?"

"Because," Joseph said, "Mary and I must stay here until we know what Jeschu plans to do. Then we will be free to return to Nazareth."

We looked at Jeschu, who was studying and not paying attention to our talk.

"Jeschu," I called out. But Mary shook her head.

"No, don't ask him."

"What, Grandmother?" Jeschu raised his head toward me.

"Your mother doesn't want me to ask you, so I can't," I told him, smiling.

Jeschu answered with his own smile. "You'll know soon enough, Grandmother, for I shall be leaving Alexandria soon. I wanted to be with the family for a while before I began my traveling."

"Traveling?" I snapped back. "You? A child? You're only sixteen, Jeschu. Where do you want to go?"

Jeschu did not answer me. Mary was silent. Joseph was silent. Ezekiel said nothing. I was the only one who ever talked. I was angry, angry because nobody ever said anything. We simply sat and waited our lives out for Jeschu. Mary remained silent, mending a garment. Joseph left the room. Ezekiel said, "If you want to, we can leave." So the decision was up to me. I had to figure out what to do. I wanted to know exactly what the boy was planning and where he was going. But Mary never asked. Joseph never said anything. The days went by, the sun set and rose, the people walked about, we ate, slept, and worked, and nothing was done. More days went by.

Jeschu found some new friends, young men I never met before. They were Egyptians, very foreign to us. What had he to do with these boys? They talked and laughed, and Mary fed them. They came in and out of the house as if it were their own. They nodded to Ezekiel and me. We did not speak their language. I did not understand them, but I did not say anything.

Jeschu was to leave soon. The thought struck fear in my heart. Where would the boy go, and what would he do?

Mary said to me to reassure me, "Don't worry, Mother. It is written. There is nothing to fear. I have always known it. Jeschu will go to foreign countries to complete his studies of people and their beliefs. No harm will come to him. He has an angel watching over him. Do you not understand that he is different from us?"

"Oh, yes," I told her. "I understand that. Of course I understand that. He doesn't need to travel, though. He could sit here and travel in his imagination."

Mary agreed. "That is true. I am sure he can go anywhere he wishes. But then the people could not know him or be with him. Jeschu wants to travel so that he can learn from different people, understand them, and teach them what he knows."

After Mary left the room, I wondered why I was so concerned about a young man who knew a trade, who was a rabbi, who knew what was going to happen before it happened, and who was very old in wisdom and understanding.

Then I answered myself, "There are robbers, murderers, dark nights, and loneliness. I am sure he will be very lonely. I do not understand how Mary can let him go and not be worried about him."

But the day came when Jeschu said he would be leaving. His mother sewed a gold coin into his robe and packed a knapsack for him. He kissed us all goodbye, saying, "I do not need this gold piece. I shall only give it away."

Mary again said nothing, for if that was what he wished to do, he would do it. We watched him leave, going with him to the harbor of the Great Sea where he boarded a boat. We went with him onto the boat.

"Come back," I said. I reached up and planted a kiss on his cheek.

"Grandmother, do not be so sad. I will come back to Nazareth. When I can, I will send you tidings by travelers and merchants." Then he added very softly, "In my heart I will always speak to you."

This scene often returns to my eyes. Mary never even cried. Joseph, of course, would not cry. Ezekiel wouldn't either. But silent tears dropped from my eyes. Thoughts reverberated in my head: my own grandson disappearing, God knows where or for how long. Who had need of one who was destined, of whom it was written that he was to become the Messiah? I shuddered at the word. If he were the Messiah, as Mary and Joseph seemed to believe, would he not be acting and speaking as a prophet? Would he not be going among the people warning them as Isaiah did? What kind of messiah is a carpenter who travels to different countries?

True, he had gifts beyond my imagination, but then he could be the son of a magician. It may be that he was taught by a stroke of fate all that magicians know, as well as the secret teachings of the Egyptians, which go back beyond the time of Moses. Now he was to be a gypsy, a wanderer, a man we might never see again.

He had wrought no miracles. He had not brought the Hebrews together as a nation. He had not persuaded the Essenes to live together with the Pharisees or the Sadducees as harmonious people.

Ezekiel didn't answer me when I asked him if he thought Jeschu was the Messiah. He said he did not know. He did not know God's ways. He did not know what God required of

Jeschu, but he agreed that up to this time, he did not seem to be the Messiah.

I decided that Jeschu was an ordinary man with some extraordinary gifts. By taking himself across the world into foreign nations, I thought he would make himself more peculiar than ever.

This was too much for Ezekiel and me. "It is time for us to return to Bethlehem," Ezekiel told me when we were alone, preparing to sleep. "Our work here is finished, and I would like for us to have some time once again in our own home."

"I think we can all leave," Joseph said the next morning when we told him we were going. "If Mary agrees, we will return to Nazareth and Bethlehem and wait there for Jeschu. We have no reason to stay in Alexandria."

We planned to go by boat this time into the closest port near Jerusalem. There would be no long desert walk. Ezekiel and I were too old and tired. We did not need to run in secret any longer.

Our trip on the Great Sea en route was uneventful and pleasant, but I was too concerned about Jeschu, alone in a strange world he knew nothing about, to enjoy the voyage. I would be concerned and sad until Jeschu came home.

CHAPTER IX

JESCHU RETURNS

We had not heard from Jeschu in the five years since he left us in Alexandria. We were waiting to hear his voice, to know he was safe and would be returning to our hearts and home. How could we even think he might not come back when he promised us to return? We would wait until he came through the door, and then we would be finished with waiting.

The boy would now be a man of twenty-one years, a seasoned traveler and a young rabbi, ready to begin his life in earnest. I was not sure Jeschu would return, but Mary said she heard from him in her head and that he was coming back soon, very soon.

Herod the Great died. I am told the three strangers who came to us long ago and gave us the gold had first gone to Herod to learn where they could find the newborn Messiah.

"I am most interested to honor him, but I do not know where he is," Herod had told them. "Please let me know where he is when you return to Jerusalem, so he may be given due honor."

But the three strangers did not return. They learned the tetrarch wanted to find the baby and slaughter him because he would claim the crown, and so they left the country without seeing him again. That is when the old tetrarch ordered all boy infants of the Essene faith to be slaughtered. Now another Herod, Herod Antipas, was in power.

The Romans became more and more brutal. Where would we go, I wondered, when the taxes become too great and the brutality unbearable? Where could we hide? Why could we not live in peace among the Romans?

Ezekiel was happy to be back in Bethlehem. I was happy, too. The house remained undisturbed, with my carpets where I had left them. My husband planted his garden and established his routine just as if he had never left. I did not have such feelings.

"I cannot believe I am an old woman," I said to Ezekiel. "We have both outlived our time for death. I want us not to die until we see our grandson once more."

"You cannot change your time for death, and you cannot make Jeschu come, my one love," Ezekiel said. "I, too, hope to live until he returns and brings us news of his travels. I also accept this may not be possible."

My husband's sweet face imprinted itself in my heart. Suddenly I knew his time would be soon. He would leave me. My heart lurched into my throat. I came to him and put my head upon his lap. "My beloved, never did I dream to have such a sweet lover as you, a confidante, one to give me such goodness and kindness. Such men are not in this world.

You must be an angel, too. Know that if you leave me first, you take with you my heart of love."

Those words were almost the last Ezekiel ever heard, because he left his body within the week. He never said he was not well. The day he departed, he worked outside in his garden, fed our goat, and ate a dinner of roast lamb made with herbs and sauce. We spent the evening outside in quiet, listening to the sounds the earth brings: the howl of a mountain animal, the cluck of roosting fowl. As the sky darkened into night, for a while the sounds increased in chorus and then, slowly, they died down.

"Nature is a good mother," Ezekiel remarked. "There is order and a place for every animal, bird, insect, even snakes. They serve just as we do. I marvel at the miracle of life."

I looked up into the hills and again wondered about the child brought into this world in some miraculous way. Jeschu was like no other human. That I knew. After a while, we went inside and shared our bed. We held each other close as we always had.

Ezekiel died in his sleep. He left his body so quietly I did not know he was gone until I awakened in the morning. The lifeless form was not my husband. But I lay there holding him while the tears fell. "Goodbye, my darling, darling one. My soul, my life. I shall see you soon again for I will never leave you. Never."

Joseph, bless him, attended to the services and prayers to be said for the dead. Mary did not say this death had been written. She cried with genuine sadness that her beloved father had left.

Mary now longed to be with her son. Never one to talk, she came to my house to keep me from loneliness, and we shared our sadness for the lost husband and father and the missing son and grandson. Mary lived in Nazareth with Joseph and Jeschu's half-brothers. I wondered if Mary had ever been with her husband in an intimate way. There was a time when I was sure my daughter was in love with Joseph and had become his wife. But I could not tell. Joseph, of course, would never confide such information to us. Mary never spoke of such subjects, or of the archangel Michael, or of her dreams.

There was no word of Jeschu. It had been a year since we asked our rabbi when he was in Jerusalem to pass the word along to other rabbis from all parts of our world so that we might learn if anyone had seen or spoken to our grandson.

When he returned to Bethlehem, Rabbi Kahane shook his head and said, "I have heard nothing. I would like to see this boy before I die. So when will he be coming to Bethlehem?"

Was Jeschu still alive as Mary said he was? What was he doing? Why did he not send some kind of message? We heard nothing.

Joseph, too, passed away. He had suffered a long time from heavy breathing and deep coughs. I think they started in Alexandria from inhaling the foul air. Mary and I both felt we had lost our anchors, our protectors. We worked harder now, tending our gardens and milking goats with the help of maidservants. The days passed in a loneliness we shared while hoping at the same time Jeschu would come to brighten our lives and give us more purpose.

The part I am going to talk of now is painful to me, almost too painful to speak about. It is the part that I have waited to tell. I would that I could run and not say it; I am a simple woman and this is a big burden to carry. My daughter,

Mary, accepted it all. As she said, it was meant to be. I do not know what Ezekiel would have said.

Mary was in Nazareth when Jeschu came to my door in Bethlehem, ten years from the day he left us in Alexandria. He came back white-robed, in sandals, bareheaded, speaking strangely in a husky voice. I did not know him. He looked like a weary traveler. When the stranger came to my door and told me who he was, I held him to my breast as if he were a child. Then I looked into his face to see that he was no longer the same as he had been when he left. Something had happened within his body and soul. He no longer reflected a man of flesh; he had become an emanation of light. I felt as if a fire had entered me. I pushed him from me. "Jeschu," I cried, "what have you done?" My eyes filled with tears of concern.

"Don't cry, Grandmother," Jeschu said. But his eyes were filled with tears. He cupped my face in his hands.

"Oh, I can see it all," I said. "I cannot bear it for you." He understood what I meant, for at that moment I knew that he was the Messiah.

I brought this man, my grandson, into the kitchen for milk and figs. The feeling of his awesome luminescence faded from me and once more he was my Jeschu. We sat at the table for a long time, but we said very little. It was enough that I could be with him and look at his face. He became more and more human to me and less like a god, more my grandson and less a foreigner who had come to my gate disguised as a holy traveler.

We went to find Mary, crossing the fields and taking a path past the village into the hills until we came to her place. She lived alone, her little house swept clean and the yard filled with animals. Mary brought a great cat with her from Egypt whose huge gold eyes turned upward in a slant, the strangest I have ever seen in a cat. He glided around the house, a yellow and black creature.

"He's human. He watches everything we say and do. Maybe he passes judgment on us," Ezekiel once said.

Mary named him Aiah.

When Jeschu and Mary saw each other, there were flashes like a current going between them. It was as if a sheet of silver flooded out of each, met in the center, and receded back to them.

Mary's eyes, too, flooded with tears when she saw Jeschu. Then when she embraced him, they shone like stars.

"My son," she said, "it is good to have you back. It is so very good." I, of course, began crying again, as if all the tears I had ever held back in my life were going to flood me out of the house. I wished I could control my weeping. But I could not.

I moved away from Mary and her son and went outdoors. Aiah stared at me with his head to one side, curious to know why I cried. I finally dried my eyes. How to explain to Aiah that these tears expressed joy, not sadness? I gave him a smile and looked to see if the goat was also wondering about me. The goat never noticed me. He occupied himself with chewing grass.

When I stepped back into the kitchen, Mary came to me and put her arm around my waist. Then Jeschu put an arm around each of us, and we just stood looking at each other, smiling, while tears filled my eyes once more.

"Oh, it is so good to see you again," I choked up and whispered. "I didn't know if we ever would."

"I have prayed for this moment," Jeschu answered. "To be in Bethlehem and Nazareth, to be home, although I have never been here before."

"But you always knew what was happening here? You knew when Ezekiel died, did you not? And when Joseph died?"

Jeschu answered, "Yes, yes, I knew. I would have returned to you then, but it was not time. I still had work to do.

"I want to know about all the things you did," I said.

"He will tell us, Mother, in time. Let us just be together now."

Mary had said nothing of her own feelings while Jeschu had been away. I marveled at her restraint and quietness. It did not seem human to me. I knew she had to have been lonely for Jeschu, especially after Joseph's death. But she would not burden Jeschu with that. I wished again, as I did so often, that I could have had her calm, quiet acceptance of whatever happened, but it was impossible for me. I could not help the way I felt or keep from showing it.

We supped and talked, saying very little of our feelings. I was fascinated by a change in Mary's attitude to Jeschu. He was no longer her son but a man, a most holy man. When I saw the two of them together, a wordless feeling welled up inside me. I asked myself, "By what power in my own body and in the loins of Ezekiel could I have produced such a daughter, and she such a son?" Indeed the Lord had spoken, and there was within these two a spark of the miraculous.

Thinking this once again sent me into a flood of tears. A messiah in the family was too much for me, the path too far from me. Jeschu was born to very humble people, not to a wealthy family who might have proclaimed him and with their wealth created a background worthy of a messiah. No, we were poor and simple, austere people. What had we to do with miracles and messiahs?

But looking back on Jeschu's strange birth and remembering the visit of those three men, the gold that eased our lives, the strange trip to Egypt, Jeschu's leaving, none of these happenings was ordinary or the ways of simple people. No, a hand of fate had surely turned and tumbled us. Where we would go and what might happen to us would not be destined by our will, it seemed, but by a higher will. Were we dice to be tossed and then thrown away? That was what Mary and Jeschu must have been saying when they said, "It is written."

In the passing days, Jeschu took his place in the village. He wore the simple robe of a teacher, and he was welcomed by our new rabbi, for Rabbi Kahane had died. But Jeschu chose to be known as a carpenter and let the people know he would do simple carpentry work in our village for the time being.

I invited Jeschu to stay in my house, for I had more room than Mary. Then it was decided that Mary would give up her house and both she and Jeschu would move into mine. Mary brought her goat, her cat, her hens, and other little animals. Once more my house was filled with life and young people who came to visit Jeschu and talk with him about his travels.

Many evenings we sat long into the night listening to Jeschu. I did not know whether what he was saying was true or whether it was fancy, for we thought it impossible that he had walked and traveled by ship and moved so far into places unknown to us and to our world.

"You think," he said, "that this world governed by the Romans is all the world there is, but there lie beyond us countries ancient in comparison to ours and rich in tradition and wisdom. Nothing seems to be known of them there."

Jeschu called one by a strange name, India. It was there that he traveled and once more studied with wise men. He then moved far away into lands I cannot name, always listening, talking, teaching, and learning. He described people of a different race, people who did not speak, people who lived to a very, very old age high up in the mountains and knew no other people but their own and did not know that the Romans or the people of India existed.

Jeschu traveled north into empty lands, he said, and into a continent that had no name. It was summer and easy to move about, but in the winter he found himself lost in snows. He said he was rescued by some small brown people who walked with him until he found himself in the sun and warmth again. Here the people wore no clothes but covered themselves with fur skins when it was cold.

As I recall it, he said he moved further and further south teaching the people about Jehovah. He healed their sores and wounds. He taught them how to pray and how to put honor in their words. He taught them about the stars, and he marveled at their own sun worship and rituals, so similar to those of the pagans.

Jeschu said he learned certain signs and hand movements that all men understood, enabling him to converse with strangers until he learned their words. He used the circle to demonstrate his meaning many times, drawing it with a stick upon the ground. The people thought he was a sun god because of his color. I am sure that people were attracted to him, drawn to him by the magnetism of his powerful aura of love.

Jeschu seemed to have traveled the world, although it was not accepted that the world existed past the Roman Empire. We believed that if a person went far enough, he would simply fall off the earth into empty space.

How Jeschu found his way back to us I could not understand, but now I know that he could move his body through his will to whatever place he wished to be. He could have returned to us any time he willed to do it.

We once spent the entire night listening to Jeschu's tales of the people and of the children of the people who, he said, were innocent and beautiful and trusting. Jeschu loved children as Mary and I did. Their honesty and their closeness to God made them vulnerable and beautiful, he said, as a flower was beautiful.

And that was the way I saw Jeschu, vulnerable and beautiful. I could not understand then that he had chosen his life, and he could have changed its course any time he decided to do so.

He stayed in Bethlehem a month, resting, saying very little to anyone other than his friends. At gatherings he held in the house he spoke of what he had seen and learned in his travels and in his studies. This was strange, indeed, for carpenters and rabbis did not do such things.

Rabbis gathered in the synagogues for prayers and rituals, prayers in praise of God, prayers for separate events in the history of the Hebrews, and special holy day prayers. The men sat separate from the women, and the women were not permitted to listen to the rabbis except for the prayers. But Jeschu said there was no difference between men and women when they prayed and learned, that they should not be made to sit separate, and woman was not the evil temptress that tradition said she was.

Jeschu sat among us, men and women. Everyone found places on the floor, a chair, or a bench, and sipped wine or hot brews of herbs while listening to him, the teacher. He did not have us recite prayers, but talked with us about our temptations and appetites. While he talked, a power of light and love emanated from him that overwhelmed us all.

The Essenes of Bethlehem had not known Jeschu as a child, but a few remembered why we had not returned. There had been some talk then about his birth and the claim in Bethlehem that he was the Messiah, but I am sure Jeschu never heard of it. If he did, he did not pay attention to it. The Essenes and Jeschu's followers would not, I believe, have questioned it if the rabbis of Jerusalem had proclaimed Jeschu the Messiah. I believe they would have agreed with them because of his powers and his illumination. But they did not proclaim him the Messiah themselves.

Our own rabbi treated Jeschu with deep respect and spent many late hours with him, but he disapproved of the things Jeschu spoke about. "My boy," the rabbi said in front of Mary and me, "you cannot change the world. You cannot go against the holy teachings of Moses. You cannot say that man can create his own destiny or change his life. He is to obey his master and the master rewards him. Look at Job. How do you explain Job?"

Jeschu smiled. "You explain him, Rabbi. He obeyed the laws."

CHAPTER X

JESCHU AS TEACHER

Jeschu spoke to groups with feeling and from the depth of his learning. But he could not reach the hearts of his listeners.

"I don't even reach their minds," he said once after a long discussion on a sunny afternoon. "People are too used to doing what the rabbis tell them to do. These holy men control and insist that their people obey the commandments or else be punished for blasphemy or be excommunicated. I want those who follow me to learn what it means to think and to love. Let their hearts be pierced with a love of life and learning. Let them discover the power they have been given to create. Let them feel it and share it."

Crowds gathered wherever Jeschu spoke. Educated in the Hebrew tradition or not, poor or rich, they hungered to be near him, to follow him, and listen to his words. But they could not apply or even understand what he talked about. None gave thought as to whether the words he spoke were true or false or in the orbit of their world. Who dared to question or oppose Jeschu as a rabbi, an authority?

Jeschu wanted more than anything to implant a habit of questioning and thinking. He spoke in words his followers could understand and in parables to instill a vivid imprint. As often as his voice rang through woods and hills, his deepest and most effective work came from teaching the people the power of silence or the path of inner awakening. Silent meditation gave the deepest rewards to the few with the ability to penetrate their hearts and hear the truth of their feelings hidden there.

Jeschu put his true teachings in code, giving each word two meanings, one for those not ready to hear and one for the true seekers who must have access to the secret code to understand. Besides using codes, Jeschu spoke in Aramaic.

Jeschu once gathered a group of his most dedicated and devoted followers. He sat them down in a ring in my house in Bethlehem. "Hold hands," he said, "and do as I say."

I looked at him to see if he wanted to include me. He motioned with his hands that I was to sit down, too. Mary sat between two of his followers, Marith and Hannah. I was seated between Peter and John. All of his closest followers had joined the ring.

The force of Jeschu's eyes pierced me until I no longer could think of anything. The force seemed to lift me off the floor. It was the same for all of us. We listened to Jeschu as if we were listening to Jehovah.

We sat for a long time. I do not know how long. Finally, Jeschu opened his eyes. He had closed them once we were still. He said, "I have a message for you. It is the most important message I could give you. I want you to listen with every individual thought you have in your body and mind. This is what I want you to hear and never forget. Never!" His eyes literally blazed with the light within his body. I was riveted to my seat, and my mind had completely entwined with my grandson's.

"The truth I teach," Jeschu said, "is within every person born of man, hidden within the heart. Man has dual consciousness. The heart conceals one consciousness. The other, the mind consciousness, is a denial of the heart. The confusion of being both eternal and temporal tears at the peaceful existence of mind with heart until a person is forced to find truth within the self. How sad that man has not been able to learn and live this magnificent truth.

"If you live as I tell you, you will never suffer the agony of lessons from teachers of the earth, but you will live as a free person who dares to be yourself complete.

"While you live on earth, become true and honest and real. That is your only mission. Do not pretend to be more than you are. Do not be less than you are. Be your own teacher. Learn to explore what you are by seeing what the consequences of your acts are upon others. Remember, you are complete as you are. You will never be less than you are today, and you will never be more than you are tomorrow. You are perfect for your task. Fulfill it, and then you will see what a change comes into your life.

"The real way to live on earth is to place life in your eyes and keep it there. The life you carry in your eyes is life everlasting. It comes from your heart. When you put it in your eyes, you are concentrating and listening and giving attention to those who are with you. But when you go into your thoughts of the mind, you lose that connection.

"When your heart is placed in your eyes, you cannot be evil, cruel, or distant. Why then are you afraid to expose yourself? The answer is in your judgment of yourself. If you feel unworthy of another's love, it shows in your eyes. But if you feel worthy to be the real person you are, then your eyes give life to all who come to you. Your love overflows as a river overflows its banks when too full. You will have your own love and your own life, and you will never suffer from the feeling that you are alone and unloved. You cannot suffer if you have your heart in your eyes."

Mary, listening, responded to Jeschu by smiling at him. She had become even quieter than she usually was. Yet her eyes reflected the life and love Jeschu spoke of because she brought warmth and love to all who came near her. I watched the two of them, my beloved children, and knew they had an unearthly connection with each other, a heart connection.

My heart was still ruled by my head, I thought. "To feel that heart consciousness you talk about, Jeschu, I must feel pain. Why would I do that?"

Jeschu, his eyes too bright and his heart too big, answered, "Grandmother, you live in your heart."

"And not my head? I am too practical. I cannot follow my heart with the kind of faith you have, Jeschu. I am too afraid. I would never make a good follower because I cannot lose my thinking."

"You do not need to learn what you already know," my grandson continued. "You are concerned for all people. It is possible to live with your feelings and still doubt with your thoughts. Thoughts bring understanding of the power of love. Pretending love through the mind denies the heart, because it does not feel. The mind rebels, but it must surrender to the heart consciousness if man is ever to know peace."

Again the tears flowed. Ezekiel, my husband, my love, my heart. Had Ezekiel found eternal life? I knew he waited for me. We were twin souls, I was sure. He would guide me when I leave this world. The years would pass. Soon my body would be put back into the earth, and my soul would be free to join Ezekiel.

Mary saw where my mind had gone. "Mother, it's time for us to prepare for our meal. How many will stay, do you think?" She put me to the task of counting those waiting outside of our house to eat with us and then to listen to Jeschu or meditate with him.

Jeschu's hands brought healing to all who came to him. He brought my own health into a perfection I never believed possible. Yet he did not go among the people in our village and heal them. His hands placed upon the forehead of a child would bring the little one's health back, but I could do no more than recommend Jeschu to them. The villagers preferred to heal themselves with herbs or call their rabbi or another healer they knew.

Aiah, Mary's cat, became ill from eating something. He lay silent and unmoving for two days after he heaved the food or poison. Mary became so concerned she went searching for Jeschu. She found him in the center of a crowd of people sitting in a circle at the foot of the hills my daughter so loved. She walked through the crowd and interrupted him. "Jeschu, please come home. I'm afraid Aiah is dying. I know you can help him."

Jeschu nodded. "I'll follow you home when I am finished."

We had not seen Jeschu for more than a week. I rejoiced that he was coming to the house and prepared some favorite foods of his. He particularly liked a thick soup of meat and vegetables seasoned with spices. I made fresh bread and took out some preserved fruit.

Mary held Aiah's head in her lap and in her soft voice murmured words I did not recognize.

Jeschu walked into the room. I thought our lamps had been lit up, he brought so much light with him. He joined his mother and Aiah on the floor.

"Aiah," he said, as if Aiah understood Aramaic. "You must arise. Get up. Your illness has been taken away. You are free to move and be yourself. Do not ever eat anything again except what is given you in this house."

Aiah's eyes opened. His head reached up to receive the touch of Jeschu. He stared at him as if he would like to say something. Instead, he shook his head and then sprang up and went to his bed.

"He's well," I said, not knowing what to say.

Mary got up as Jeschu did. "You will stay for supper?"

Jeschu hesitated, looking first at his mother and then at me. I knew he wanted to leave, but I wanted him to stay, to share a few minutes with his family. "I will," he said.

We brought him a fresh robe. He bathed and combed his hair. Then we shared food and talk for an hour.

"I must go," he said, rising from the table. "I'd forgotten how much I enjoy my two mothers and my home. I will return soon to spend more time with you."

If Jeschu was not recognized for his healing, he was well known for his ability to settle disputes among neighbors. Men came to him during an argument and asked for his opinion. It is strange that Jeschu, so gifted and so wise, spent his time settling ridiculous disputes such as who should go to the well for water when men work together. Going after the water was a woman's job, and the men were ashamed to go to the well. They argued about whose turn it was or why it should be that one of them must do this. So they came to Jeschu for his opinion. I listened.

Jeschu said, "Do your own bidding. If you are too proud to carry the water, then do not carry it. And if all of you are too proud to carry water, then you will see the consequences. Therefore, what is there to argue about?"

The men walked away silently. It took them time to realize what Jeschu had pointed out. By doing so they began to think a little. Yet they did not attribute wisdom to Jeschu. They were puzzled by him. He gave them such strange answers.

Mary and I laughed between ourselves when we heard this discussion. We thought it a very wise answer, which did not put the burden of getting the water on anyone. The men had to decide which was more important, pride or water.

One day Mary and I went visiting with Jeschu to the home of some friends who lived some distance away. Their names were Sela and Matthias.

We walked a good two hours in the hot sunshine to their house. Matthias welcomed us, showing great pleasure, honored to have us as guests.

We sat in a cool, dark room. Sela and Matthias both had red hair and blue eyes. They did not look like Semites. They did not come from our part of the country. I don't know where they came from. It was some area connected with Rome, I believe, but they had been living in Bethlehem for a number of years. They met Jeschu through another friend and invited us to spend the day with them.

Matthias was a fisherman. He said he went to the Sea of Galilee and sometimes to the Great Sea to fish but then was gone for long days. This made Sela unhappy. They had two small children, wide-eyed and beautiful. I held one and Mary held one. They jumped down to climb over Jeschu. We were very happy with the children and with the cold milk, figs, and grapes we were offered.

Matthias told Jeschu, "I'm interested in studying with the Essenes, to learn to live with their laws. I have read their scrolls. I like what they say. But tell me, why is there such disagreement among the sects when they also disagree among themselves? Why do they disagree and fight with each other? And why do you not join them when you are a rabbi and can show the people your beliefs?"

I looked at Jeschu. He did not answer immediately but thought a while. Then he said, "There are three branches of a tree. Which is growing faster? Which is not needed by the tree? Shall one be dispelled and will that bring the other two together? These branches of Judaism grow for a purpose. Out of them, human beings understand their own pathways to greater degrees.

"We are none of us on the same path or walking the same way. Thus the three branches are the three tribes or sects, the three branches of Judaism, and this is how they must grow. None will reach the Kingdom of Heaven before the other. It is the fruit of the tree, the individual, who reaches the Kingdom of Heaven and not the limbs of the tree. The tree will produce its life while sometimes the branches die. Then how can they be one?"

Matthias was satisfied and said, "So then if I choose the Essene branch, it is because that is what I understand and the way I wish to grow?"

Jeschu agreed with a nod, and then Matthias said, "Why do you eat meat when the Essenes do not permit the eating of meat? And why do you drink wine when the Essenes do not permit the drinking of wine? And why do you stay separate from them when you are a rabbi and can teach in a synagogue?"

Jeschu answered: "I too am a vine and I live from the root of my father's vineyard. The ways of the Essenes are not mine, for I have a way of teaching and a path, a way of growing that is not like the Essenes' and not like any other branch. I am fed from the food of my father's vineyard."

Matthias pursued the argument. "But why do you eat meat? Do you believe in eating meat? Do you believe in drinking wine?"

Jeschu answered, "These are the rules and laws of man and not of God. It is truth that God calls the fruit of man. It is love that produces truth. What has it to do with what a man eats? If a man finds truth, what matter that he eats of meat and bread and wine? These are food for man so long as he wants them. When he does not, they are no longer necessary for him, just as hunger for truth itself begins as a seed and develops into a growth so powerful it can encompass the world. The seed is forgotten in the plant."

I did not follow all of what Jeschu said, though I understood some, but when I listened I was filled with great joy, for at last I heard him speak out. I treasured his words.

I knew that Jeschu would be leaving us soon and that he would be prepared at that time to go wherever his destiny was to take him. The foreboding covered me in darkness. I did not want to think of it. The clouds came into my eyes. I did not want Jeschu to see them.

I looked to Mary for comfort, but Mary's eyes were bright and shining. She had no clouds in them, for she never doubted the path of Jeschu. Perhaps in truth she knew its end. I did not. I did not want to know.

People arrived to see the man who, it was whispered, was the young Messiah. Between the villagers and the fishermen, I was told, they said, "There is one in Nazareth who is wise, but he will be in trouble. He is breaking the laws we must obey, and he will be brought before a tribunal sooner or later."

"They expect you to be brought before the high priests in Jerusalem for breaking the Mosaic law," Matthias told Jeschu.

On our way home I asked Jeschu what Matthias meant. "Surely," I said, "you have the right to teach what you believe to be in truth."

Jeschu looked at me and put his arms around my shoulders. He said, "Grandmother, there are few who know God's laws. There are many who define them, and there are others who enforce them, and that is their work. They do not stop to perceive the truth of the laws or attempt to understand them. Therefore, our teachings have become distorted and twisted until they are an authority for obedience rather than laws for peaceful sharing of life among ourselves. Some day these laws will no longer be necessary. Every man will know his truth and let his neighbor speak his own, and the law will be within the heart of man and not outside."

"That's a long day in coming," I said. "A long day in coming. But if you speak so and you break the law, how will you be able to help others? For you will be tried and stoned, and that will be the end of you."

Jeschu smiled. He took his arm from my shoulders and put my hand in his own. "Grandmother, you have spent all these years worrying about your grandson, yet there has never been a time or a place where any of your worries changed one bit of my life. Times are coming when you will see me suffer. Try not to worry. Try to understand that I have seen and understood the message I must give to our people. That is my mission. My mother understands. She is no longer my mother, but my friend. You, blessed one, you hold on to that fear and you will suffer. Trust and have faith in me and you will not, for you will know a glory instead."

Again tears started rolling down my face, and I cried, "I cannot, Jeschu. I cannot bear to think of you suffering. I cannot bear to think you feel you must give your life to teach men lessons they don't want to hear. What good will it do? Why do you have to do it? I know. I know it must be. I know it has to be. I know I am wrong to feel so much pain, but I cannot help it. I cannot help it. I was not born knowing like your mother. I am just a woman who bore a child who bore a son. In my heart I cannot see or understand any more than that.

"Jeschu," I pleaded with him, "don't go away. Don't teach the people. Stay here and be a carpenter and let the people come to you. You are safe here. Nothing very much can happen to you. The people will not harm you. Do what you must do here, where you are protected. Do not leave us."

"I must go, Grandmother," he answered. "I must go. I cannot say what is to happen. I am sorry for the pain you take upon your shoulders, and I pray for you, for I dearly love you."

We walked into the house tired and weary. Mary prepared a meal and came to me in my room. She put her arms around me as I continued to cry. She too had tears in her eyes. She said, "Mother, I share your tears. I, too, am human. I know your pain. But there is no way to change Jeschu. We can only help him as much as we can and pray, for he has a task to do, and he will do it."

I was still trembling. It is as if I knew that Jeschu was going to be treated cruelly on his journeys by those who were now openly jeering him. I knew someday someone would hurt him and perhaps destroy him, and he would no longer be with us.

I am taking this time to recall the events preceding Jeschu's journeys before he went to Jerusalem, for I do not wish to go into detail about them. I did not go with Jeschu but remained in Bethlehem. Mary, I know, went with him or met him in different places. During these long months of preaching, I stayed in my house and heard stories about my grandson. People in the village were of two kinds: those who were in sympathy with us, knew us well, and considered Jeschu a rabbi and teacher, and those who considered us pariahs to be shunned as transgressors of the laws of the Israelites, who considered us allied to the heathens.

The days passed quickly, and Jeschu was always in my mind as he used the house as a base from which to address his followers. His work and his name were spreading from one town to the next. He was meeting with people who were looking for a leader. He always gave people help when he could. These people would come to our house any time of the day or night to talk with the holy man, as they called him. Jeschu never seemed to need any sleep. He was up whenever anyone called his name. He explained again and again that while prayers to God were most important, real guidance and solution to a problem came from within the spirit self. They said prayers that were memorized and spoken by the people together. They wanted to get the prayer into the air to God. The prayers were made up by the rabbis, who had worked them out from the sound of the Hebrew words and letters to have a special meaning. This is what Jeschu told me, that the sound was what made the prayers important and what made them work. When the sound was rhythmic, then the work was completed and the answer would return through the same kind of rhythm from God.

Jeschu said that these prayers would always work if the people put their feelings into them. But they did not do that. They used the words and the rhythm, but they did not feel what they said, and they lost the power of the heart, which was necessary in order for a prayer to be answered.

I felt very happy to see Jeschu surrounded by followers eager to learn what he taught. But the happiness could not last very long. Word of his activities leaked out of Bethlehem and Nazareth into the surrounding towns and along the coastline. Soon talk would spread to Jerusalem. Gossip would build up until there was no truth in it. They were saying, "A rabbi in Galilee is telling people lies and teaching them heathen ways." Many times, those who were strict and uncompromising with the laws of the Israelites were angry and critical of Jeschu. But people kept coming to see him with their questions.

Rumors spread that Jeschu had been taken up like Moses and secretly given the laws of a new age. He was also supposed to have learned the laws of magic from the netherworld. This meant that he had the power to raise the dead and do all kinds of miracles. These were of the devil and to be shunned.

When Jeschu said he wanted to preach a gospel of love to people—strangers in the street—and show them how love heals, I wondered if my grandson was sane. I could not quiet my thoughts. He had been prepared in education and travel to become a leader, if not a messiah. He did not show any signs of being an important man. His plan of teaching to anyone who cared to listen, heathen or Hebrew, was more like a rabbi with no special ability wandering around performing miracles. These miracles could brand him as a magician and could cause him to be killed.

I told Jeschu, "I am truly worried, Jeschu. I wonder if you are in your right mind."

He looked at me for a long time and answered me slowly as if he were weighing each word, "You are right, Grandmother. I am not sane by the standards of this world. I am not of this world. I have ascended, as you know, and that means I am living in a world of spirit, which is eternal life. I am here to bring the gospel of love to mankind. That is not sane in your understanding, for there is no such world in the minds of men."

I didn't understand. He was in this world, and this was a real world as far as I could see. If Jeschu said he lived in an eternal world, then what was this one? It had been here a long time, and I thought it planned to remain here for a long time. Then what was he talking about? I asked him.

I learned that I had to say my own prayers to my own creator and listen to my own feelings, and then take into myself whatever feelings I had and clean out the anger I felt. Then I could pray with a clean heart. That was very hard for me to do. I did not have a clean heart. I was full of angry feelings against the people who would hurt Jeschu, criticize him and the family, and always challenge him about the law.

I understood why he would not teach obedience to the law, because law is unnecessary when a person obeys the prompting of his heart. If he carries within himself a true and loving heart, he will not steal, covet, murder, dishonor, or do anything that breaks the law of God.

But what of the synagogues and temples where the Hebrews worshiped? If Jeschu would not use a synagogue for himself but preferred to talk in the open fields, and if he considered laws unnecessary when people learned to follow the inner laws of their own consciousness, then he was defying all the traditions of Judaism. Surely those whose lives and living depended on the keeping of the tradition would not tolerate such heresy and would find a way to destroy him.

The Hebrews always believed that idol worshipers were unclean. They ate of forbidden meats and forbidden fish. They did not observe the Sabbath or the laws of Moses. Therefore, Israelites shunned them. Jeschu said these laws were to be replaced and changed, and that all men must learn to love each other. He said that this was his mission, and he would teach anyone who came to him. Our house was sometimes full of Samaritans and the heathens of our own Judaea. Hebrew and heathen spoke and shared our bread and bathed in the same waters. Such things broke an unwritten law.

"That is what is going to get him into trouble," I said to Mary. "Jeschu can teach what he likes, but he should not break the laws. If he does, he will be stoned. Why can't he talk to these people in separate groups? Why does he flout our ways, our tradition?"

"Jeschu cannot work any other way," Mary said. "If he does not do the very thing he preaches, then he is himself not in truth but lives a lie, and therefore he cannot be a true teacher of men."

"But there is such a thing as common sense," I said. "What good is it going to do him to be killed for what he thinks?"

Mary did not answer me. I knew she suspected he could be killed, and I knew she did not want me to voice such fears.

"Mother," she said, going toward the kitchen, "it is time to make bread."

We baked on Wednesdays, preparing for Friday evening when the gatherings began. No matter how many people came, there was always enough bread, milk, figs, fruit, cheeses, nuts, and wheat porridge. Many people brought food to be shared. Others helped in preparation.

If only things could go on the way they have been, I thought. I would not mind the work or the crowds or the long discussions. Jeschu and Mary were with me, and we were safe enough. I spent hours thinking of places to hide Jeschu if the people raised themselves against him.

I finally ordered a workman to dig a small cave in a field near our house and covered it so that it was completely concealed with weeds and waste. It could not be seen, and no one knew of it, outside of the workman who dug it out for me and filled it with enough supplies—dried barley, water jugs, dried fruits, and nuts—to last several days. Although the air would become stale, there was enough coming in through cracks to make it safe, and Jeschu could hide there for days without being found.

I prayed to God that it would never be necessary for him to use it, but I wanted it there. When I told Jeschu what I had done and showed him where it was, he had the kindness not to laugh or criticize me.

"That is a wonderful thing you did," he said, "and I shall not forget it, Grandmother. If the time comes when I need it, and I am close enough, you know I will come running to it." He hugged me hard. I knew he was sorry to see me so concerned and worried, but he did not let it influence him. His mission was his sole purpose, and he intended to let nothing keep him from it.

I do not think I truly understood what a strong spiritual being Jeschu was. Except for the time when he first returned and I knew in my heart that he was the Messiah, I did not think of him except as my grandson and a man of learning.

As Jeschu proceeded to give his wisdom and understanding to the people, I was able to remove some of my fear, and then I could feel what a strong and loving person he was as teacher and a rabbi. For a rabbi was more than a teacher. He was a holy man whose word was not to be questioned. He could decide for you what was right or wrong and what was good or evil. We believed he could give you forgiveness for a sin or crime and he could show you where you erred so you could repent for yourself. He was always ready to give help if a person asked for it. If you did not obey the rabbi, you were not a good Hebrew. If you were a good Hebrew, you followed the scriptures.

Jeschu changed with this work he was doing. He blossomed, opening up the way a bud becomes a flower, full and new with life. His voice changed to a deeper pitch. His eyes came alive with a glow not of this earth. I thought he had a source of energy from God because he never seemed to be tired or hungry. We took food to him every day if we knew where he was. Sometimes he ate, and sometimes he didn't. He did not seem to notice one way or another. But he would sip wine with his friends while he talked. I felt that was good for him, as wine brings roses to the cheeks, power to the tongue, and warmth to the heart. Jeschu smiled when I told him that.

"Wine," he said, "is the essence of the grape, and the grape is the fruit of the vine, and the vine is rooted in the Father's heart. If you drink of the wine, you are tasting the essence of his own heart."

That was beautiful, but I didn't believe it. Wine is wine. That was how I felt, but Jeschu did not believe in saying things were what they were. He talked with his heart and his feelings and not factually as I saw it. I wished Jeschu would start to have more common sense, like a farmer, and I kept saying that, but I knew it could not happen. "Sooner or later he will become known by the authorities of the temple. Then the world will fall in," I predicted to Ezekiel. I had developed a habit of talking to my late husband when I was alone, as if he could live in my heart.

Jeschu soon saw that the rabbis would not give his words any acceptance. This made him angry. Why was he not accepted by the Hebrews, his own people, who were waiting for the Messiah? I believe that by now Jeschu knew he was the Messiah, but he did not want to say so. He wanted people to realize it through their experiences with him.

When Jeschu spoke, he gave his heart to the people in a way they did not understand. His heart was of an energy far beyond any people had ever felt. This energy floated all around him, and soon everybody was calling each other brother, giving each other all kind of attention.

That feeling would be so good that Jeschu believed he had taught the people how to love. But after he left them, they would return to the same feelings as before, and Jeschu would feel bad. I guess I was not very helpful with his problems because I could not understand why he expected to be understood by people who could not even read the simplest kind of writing. These followers were ignorant and followed a leader like sheep. The people went on day to day, drinking wine, eating, living with their families, and gathering for special events. I am not talking about the Hebrews, but about the people who more and more followed Jeschu.

I called them sheep to Jeschu, and he told me not to do that. "These are people with the same heartbeat as your own. Their ignorance," he said, "is not from laziness but because they have not been taught. They will learn when our own people will not. They will learn what I have to teach while my own people will forget the truth and live in the past. That is what I see."

I was unhappy for Jeschu. He had a following mostly of heathens. They tried to understand what he spoke about. They could feel his loving heart and listen to his words, but they failed to apply them. Hebrews understood that Jeschu was a rabbi breaking the laws of Moses and preaching to heathens. Sometimes young boys followed him. When he was meditating alone, they threw rocks at him, then they ran away laughing.

CHAPTER XI

IN THE DESERT

One day Jeschu came into the house where Mary was baking bread. "Mother," he told her, "I have decided to go into the hills for a few days. I have thoughts to clear out."

When I heard this, fear prickled through my spine. Jeschu would have to wrestle with the facts: Hebrews did not accept his teachings, and the heathens were not ready to understand them. Why, I wondered, did he not know how to proceed if he already knew the secrets of this earth? A storm would break among them soon. I felt it in my bones. If I knew what was going to happen, surely he did, too.

Mary finished setting the dough for rising and went to pack another robe, undergarments, and a wiping cloth into a knapsack for her son. She put in bread, cheese, fruit, wine, and a flask of water.

"I shall return soon, perhaps in ten days," Jeschu said. "Do not be concerned. I must clear my mind." Mary nodded but said nothing.

Turning toward us as he was about to leave, Jeschu came back and put his arms around us both. He said no more but walked out the door.

Obsessed with worry about my grandson, I slept little and could not enjoy my food. A tightness in my throat seemed to lock it up.

Mary tried to comfort me. "Mother, please don't worry. You know he is protected by God. Everything that happens is happening through the will of God."

I couldn't believe that. "Why would God give Jeschu so much suffering? Why does he not help him? Why does he let him suffer cruelty with slurs and with people spitting at him when he passes by? The people Jeschu tries to help come to him for healing and love, but they don't give anything back. I don't understand why he wants to go around talking about God, truth and love, when the people are throwing rocks at him."

I was crying again, and I wished I wouldn't in front of Mary. I knew she worried as much as I did though she was stronger and much wiser.

Ten days later, I saw a man in the fields staggering toward the house. Was it Jeschu? Or was it a wraith weaving through the field as if he were floating? It was Jeschu. His eyes had sunk into his head, and his body was covered with dirt. He wore only a loincloth. He came closer.

"Jeschu," I cried as I ran toward him. He fell before I could reach him. I screamed for Mary. She came running, and together we carried him into the house. We brought him water and bathed him and put him into his bed while he still was not conscious. He awakened some hours later. Mary brought him milk and dates. He ate so slowly I knew he had not had food in a long time. He seemed to be far away. He looked past us, not at us, as if his thoughts were still in the desert.

"Jeschu, are you all right?" I asked him. He took my hand and squeezed it. There was no answer. Mary sat quietly. I knew she was praying the way Jeschu had taught her.

He slept through the night, not having said one word. In the morning after I dressed, I went into his room. He was awake. "I'll bring you some breakfast," I said. He shook his head no.

"Only some figs and goat's milk," I pleaded.

"I am not hungry," he said, not trying to rise from his bed. I left for the kitchen and returned with a slice of his mother's fresh bread, hot milk, and figs. I put them beside him, hoping he would just eat. Then I sat next to him, waiting for him to tell me what had happened in the desert.

Mary joined us, and we sat in silence for a long while. Jeschu did not touch the food. Then he said, "I cannot tell you what took place exactly, but I went there to pray and to get rid of anger, which has begun to be rooted in my heart. I have been angry with the rabbis and the people who jeer at me. I was not able to do anything about it. I wanted to hurt them. That is why I left. I cannot be angry and do my work. There is no anger in me now. I am rid of it. That is what I went into the desert to do."

"But, Jeschu," I said, "what are you going to do? Those people were angry with you. They did not go out into the desert to get rid of their anger. They are building more and more hatred, and they will destroy you if they can. I know it."

"They cannot destroy the seeds I plant," Jeschu answered. "They already have lost their battle. Those who learned my teachings and understand them will keep teaching even if they must hide to do it. Those who do not and those who persecute me will not be given any more problems by me. I will meet them openly, face to face, and if they destroy my body, my spirit will remain. If my spirit is taken away by God, then I will not be able to do my work on earth, but I have been promised that my spirit will remain. It is not my body, and my body cannot be taken once the life leaves it. I will claim my body and return to earth."

"Jeschu, get some rest," I said, getting up from the chair. "You must not talk anymore. You need to be quiet. You have had a hard time. After my work is done, I would like to talk again."

Mary sat with her son after I left. I felt my head rocking and reeling like a spinning ball. The house seemed filled with some kind of energy. What was wrong with me? I didn't know what to do. Surely Jeschu had gone mad. Surely the trials and tests and the days in the desert alone had been too much. I thought of calling the rabbi, but that would displease both the rabbi and Jeschu.

Jeschu was not able to talk to this new rabbi, the one who had replaced our beloved old rabbi who knew about Jeschu's birth. No, that would not work. Mary would not be concerned. She would say that Jeschu was fine. I thought of Ezekiel. What would he suggest? I didn't have an answer.

I decided to mix Jeschu a compote of herbs to put him to sleep for a day or so. Rest would help him more than anything I knew of, and maybe his exhaustion would pass.

I went to the kitchen to prepare my brew. There were secrets in herbs that had been given to me long ago. I had never put them together before, but now I did and let the herbs brew until the good substances had come out of the roots and the flowers. When Jeschu awoke, I gave him a cup disguised with honey. He slept again until the next day.

He seemed to be better. He did not talk of the problems he had with the people and with the rabbis. I was hoping he had decided to listen to what I said and give up his mission. But this was not the case. He determined that he would proceed with his work, whatever the cost. The cost was not important, he said, but the planting of the seeds, as he described it, was important.

When Jeschu decided to do something he believed he was supposed to do, no one could tell him otherwise. No one could tell him to consult other people or to think about it for a while. He knew what he was to do from some inner source I did not know about, even if it didn't make any sense to him. Even if it didn't mean what he thought it meant, he followed his intuition. We called it stubbornness when we did not agree with what was happening, and we called it persistence when we did.

Jeschu's intuition told him he would be given many trials by the people, but that in the end he would win his battle, and the people would be transformed by what he said to them. This was what he was waiting for.

Jeschu had not been told, as far as I knew, that he was a special person from birth. He thought he was the son of Joseph, the carpenter. We never told him otherwise, for we all agreed it would have given him a warped view of himself that might harm him in this life. Mary never thought it right to say anything. She felt Jeschu would be influenced to aspire to that which she had been told he was to become, the Messiah. She felt that it would put a burden on him she did not wish him to bear.

Had other people told him anything about the mystery of his birth? Jeschu never said, and I do not believe anyone did. Our friends would not, for the Essenes did not speak of such things. Those of the other sects long ago would have forgotten that old story, as they judged it to be.

The order of Herod to destroy Essene boys under the age of two months had been carried out. Its horror left a mark of pain on all people of our race. That cruelty somehow expiated whatever crime was supposed to have been committed by the birth of the Messiah, and I suppose the people presumed he had been murdered. Jeschu knew of the murder of the babies, but he had never said anything that would make us think he connected that with our escape into Egypt.

CHAPTER XII

JESCHU'S MIRACLES

Jeschu went about the countryside helping any person who reached out to him. He took away sores, painful wounds, twisted hips, crippled bodies, and lost minds of those who wandered in Galilee begging for bread. Jeschu provided bread. He provided food for their souls and gave them the courage to find their way through faith and love, and a will to survive. Dirty, uncombed, and in tatters, they followed my grandson in increasing numbers.

Jeschu talked to these lost souls, men and women with eyes turned downward into the ground. "Look up! Look up!" he liked to say as he cupped their faces in his hand. When their eyes met his, his love embraced their souls and renewed them in strength.

Many were not convinced of the cures, the healing, the talks. They said to one another, "He's a magician. Watch his hands work. He knows how to make people believe they are cured when they are not. As soon as he leaves, they go right back to their suffering."

Others, following him for weeks on end, affirmed in awe that this rabbi was a very holy man. "I see an aura of God, a strong light around his head," they said. Occasionally, I heard, or Mary told me, of some man screaming in the crowd, "Can't you see the horns of the devil rising from the head of this man who preaches to you?"

It was natural for people to feel afraid of Jeschu when he performed what they thought were miracles. They did not understand that he knew the laws of God as we did not. That was why he healed so well. He finally did his healing work in the open where people could see that when he raised his hand, a person recovered from sickness or a crippled child walked. Jeschu did much more than wave his hand, but that was all the people saw.

Jeschu did other healing work with his will when he was not with his followers. I am sure of that.

Mary said to me, "Jeschu is being pursued by crowds wherever he goes. When they see him heal a blind man with a wave of his hand, they bring him every maimed, sick, or crippled person they can find for him to heal. My son does not like to be followed by so many people, but he doesn't know how to get them to listen to his words except by doing what they consider miracles."

Jeschu said, repeating it in different words and different ways, "I am a product of love. I am created out of love. You, too, are created out of love, and you, too, will return to love, and you, too, cannot exist on earth without love.

"For love is the power giving life to all things, and love is the healing of all that is false upon the earth. When there is not love, there is not life, but only the emptiness of beliefs formed from the hungry hearts of men.

"How, then, can I show you that you can know peace and the good life on earth by not returning evil for evil? How can I show you that you can gain the world by receiving into yourself the power of love and removing from yourself the hunger for love?"

I believed that Jeschu had a wrong idea about that. He thought every family had the same kind of love we had in ours. I think he did not realize that Mary came into this world with love and life in abundance. I, myself, could not believe her perfection. She seemed to me to be less human and less at fault than Jeschu. Joseph, too, in his silence gave Jeschu love of a kind not seen on earth. We were not as good or pure as Mary and Joseph, but Ezekiel and I never crossed Jeschu or his parents.

My words were the words of a worried grandmother who cared more about her grandson than about the Messiah. I suppose that was wrong, but then I cannot say that I am sorry. I was human and so was Ezekiel. I did not believe Mary, Joseph, or Jeschu were altogether human. They came from some other world. Therefore, when Jeschu talked about the possibilities of man to his people, he did so without realizing that his life was very different from theirs, and that what he asked was almost impossible for the others to do.

Jeschu's followers spoke to me of their concern about their rabbi's habit of not eating. "He pushes away the food we bring him," they said, noting Jeschu's thin body. "He says he is fed by the Father and does not need to eat."

"There is a strong glow in his face. Maybe he does get nourished by Jehovah," a sweet-faced young boy named Laban offered.

"Nonsense," I answered. "He must have nourishment. Let me know where you are meeting, and I will bring him hot food."

Laban offered to guide me to where Jeschu was. "I can carry the food for you," he said.

When my grandson was close by, I brought him a hot meal of vegetables and meat and fruit and nuts. Laban carried the food, and we forced our way past a strange and mixed mass of men, women, boys, young girls, and dogs. Some were Hebrews, but others were from Samaria and other nearby places of heathen worship.

I came up to Jeschu and said, "Eat." Perhaps my voice conveyed panic. Jeschu stopped without finishing his sentence and turned to me. He paused for a moment, smiled, and said, "Yes, Grandmother, I will eat."

After that, I waited for Jeschu to stop talking before I brought food and stayed with him until he finished what I brought. Every time he looked up at me, he smiled. The sweetness of his smile tore at my heart. I loved him so much.

Then he continued with his work into the night. Lines of people stood waiting for him to bless them and give succor for their suffering. I wondered what lasting effect he had. He taught people to be clean, to pray, to give thanks, to ask forgiveness, and to forgive themselves. He taught them how to act with love and not to take advantage of one another.

What he accomplished with these souls hungry for some kind of peace in their hearts made him stronger. Instead of fainting from exhaustion, he became immersed in a powerful vitality, brighter and more full of life than ever. When the last supplicant disappeared down the road for the evening, Jeschu came into the house, bathed his face and hands, and undressed in order to bathe his body. Then he put on a clean robe and sat outside the house under the stars for an hour or two. He did not sleep very much.

Mary grew thinner every year. I think she still missed Joseph, for he had given her strength and courage. The loss of Ezekiel and Joseph—their deaths occurred so close together—created pain and loneliness in both of us. Their loss bound together our own souls and gave us a feeling more of being sisters than mother and daughter.

Joseph had protected Mary from people and responsibilities that ordinarily would have been hers. That is, she did not have children, and she did not do the usual work of a wife. Although she baked the bread and cooked when that was necessary, as every wife had to do, her handmaiden took care of much of the rougher cleaning work. Mary was free to work with flax and to weave the wool.

She liked doing that and she liked working with dyes, but after Joseph died and Jeschu returned, she seemed to go into an indifferent state. She became like a candlelight that flickers. The flame spreads its light, oh so softly, but there is one power behind it, and it seems that any moment it will go out. I felt that way about Mary, that she could at any moment let go of her flicker of life. That is why I speak of her as being silent. In a very silent way, she brought light and comfort to us. When she was around, her very presence was like a flame of love. Jeschu and Mary were more like twin spirits than mother and son. On the other hand, Mary was stronger than she seemed to be, and she denied what I felt about her.

Jeschu, too, did not, in one sense, seem to be a grandson, for he was not of this world. He did not have the feelings of a man who was hungry for wife, children, and a house. He had no thought of these things that I know of. There were girls in the village who looked at him with interest. I also looked at them with interest. I would have been overjoyed if Jeschu had brought home a robust maiden for a wife and given us another child. But I knew within my heart that this was not to be and that Jeschu himself was not made of the kind of flesh that finds its satisfaction in sexual expression, lovemaking, or carrying on the responsibilities of a family. I had always known that Jeschu would not be such a person.

Jeschu had always existed in another sphere, another plane of existence. He communed with his own God, whoever he was, for I do not know that it was Jehovah, who is my God. Jeschu saw him in another way, as if he had a guiding star and that star was his Father, and that star was God, and that star walked with him.

That is why I often questioned whether Jeschu was mad. For who can talk to a star and who can talk to God? Was he Moses? Sometimes I said yes. He was far more beautiful and far more real than Moses could have been. His beauty shone in him, his glory enveloped him, and sometimes I could even see it. But most of the time I experienced it as a certain blissful relaxation when he walked into the room, for there was light whenever he appeared.

Other times I did not see him like this, and my mind was on the details of daily life—tasks and duties such as preparing food, cleaning the house, growing vegetables and fruit, work and caring for the family. I did not speak of these things to Jeschu. He was concerned with bigger issues: "It is false to force women into subservience to another person and to make a man subservient. Why do men feel they must have privileges not given to women? Why can women not learn to read, write, and think? Do they not have the same spirit in them as men?"

Occasionally, when he felt too much put upon by the people, Jeschu retreated to the Essene cave that his father, Joseph, attended at times. There he went into a retreat of fasting and prayer and came out renewed and cleansed. While Jeschu was gone, the people scurried about like so many ants who had lost their bearings and had no place to go. They wandered aimlessly, asking when Jeschu would return. What they were looking for was the gift of his healing and his company to give them sustenance and solace. I would have liked to believe that such a crowd of people could be changed by words, but I knew it would take a bolt of lightning or Jehovah himself appearing in the heavens with his fists thundering at them to change them, for they were nearer to being animals with their lust, their crudity, and their cruelty. Could such be changed by words? Jeschu believed that they could. He believed that his love would bring into the world a new consciousness of the meaning of the word. Of the people who came to him, very few were his own Hebrew brothers and sisters.

Where were his people? A few Judaeans were with Jeschu constantly. A few followed his teachings rather than those of their own rabbi. I was troubled for them, for I knew that they, too, would be charged with breaking the Judaic laws and be punished. Then what would happen to all their love? Would they love those who put them to death with stones? Would they love their rabbis who decreed their death or banished them from their congregation? Would they abandon

Jeschu? I believed that was what they would do. Who has the courage to stand alone and not deny himself when stones are flying at him? Jeschu was not afraid to die. But his followers had lust and hunger, and they wanted to feed upon animals and live like animals. They took in Jeschu's words, muttered to themselves, and worked to learn what he said. But could one teach faith to such?

Jeschu's patience was greater than mine. I could not go and listen as Mary often did when he talked. For it made me ill to see my grandson, who communed with his own God, stand before these people who were little more than animals, to give them the beauty of his words. The rabbis should have been listening and honoring my grandson.

Who were these rabbis? Jeschu, in his retreat, spent much time with Essene rabbis in Galilee. They did not dispute his teachings for they, too, were wise men and understood the importance of what he said. But they did not go out among the people to talk to them. They lived, worked, ate, and prayed among themselves.

Ezekiel and I, along with many people in Nazareth and Bethlehem, had left the Essenes because we wanted to live as a family. But the choice had been ours. We could have remained in the caves of the Essenes for a lifetime, living in their ways without being disturbed by the Sadducees, the Pharisees, the Zealots, Romans, the pagans, or strangers roaming through Judaea and our countryside. We could have lived in peace with our own creed, for no one would have disturbed us. Jeschu could have lived in those caves himself for his lifetime, studying, learning, and teaching those who came and truly desired to learn. His philosophy was based upon the teachings of the Essenes. It was truth as they knew it and as Jeschu knew it.

But Jeschu believed the time had come when these people could begin to perceive the truth, the gospel, the news that they were not living in order to satisfy their needs, but instead were the glorious creation of God and therefore emissaries of his light and his love. Jeschu understood well the risks he took in bringing these words to the masses. He said, "To sacrifice a lamb is to give up something that is a possession. But to give up by choice, through the will and the heart, is another step not requiring the sacrifice of a lamb."

Around this time Mary, too, would never eat if I did not remind her. She, too, lapsed into hours of silent prayer and meditation. I knew not what this love of God was, mingled with a love and faith in life. Yet, I suspected that she grieved to see Jeschu so thin, to see him going out bravely with crowds of people who had no respect or dignity, who quarreled among themselves, who ate crudely, spat, and defecated like animals. One would think that Jeschu would have turned from such people. But he did not see them, I suppose. He saw only the blindness of their souls. He beckoned them to his heart. Could it be that he pierced them and changed them with his own power? I would not be surprised, for he had the power. When he was utterly emptied of his power again, he would retreat into the caves and come back renewed, filled once more with his glory.

Jeschu often walked back to the house through a path in the woods. I see him in my mind's eye as he was then, his long black hair in ringlets, his eyes blazing blue, his skin pale, pale white, his body thin to emaciation, his robe hanging loosely from his body, his feet in sandals, his hands long fingered, and oh so quiet. It seemed that a breeze could blow him away. I saw him walking along this path when suddenly five men fell upon him, beat him with a thong, and called him names. They told him to cease his preaching or worse would happen. They left him there bleeding and beaten. No one was around. I saw him in my mind's eye because I felt every blow myself.

He came into the house. I washed his wounds and cried my agony to him. "Will you stop this torment? Will you stop this torture?"

"These were not Hebrews who stoned me," he said, as I washed out cuts on his arms and face. "These were men who swear I am the devil. They try to stop the crowds from listening. But they did not harm me."

I believe this was the incident that made Jeschu decide to go to Jerusalem and present his teachings and learning to the rabbis in all humility and ask for their consideration, so what he had seen and known and the glory promised could be accepted. He did not use the word *messiah*, but he didn't have to. Jeschu undoubtedly was an emissary of God with a mission in his soul, and it was inevitable that he go to Jerusalem and face the rabbis there.

At this point Jeschu took long walking trips through Galilee to Caesarea, Capernaum, Judaea, and Bethsaida. The people came from the north, the south, from Idumea, from Samaria, and Judaea. When Jeschu went to Judaea to talk to people in the hills, large crowds followed him in the hope that they would see a miracle for themselves.

Stories of Jeschu's words and actions reached Jerusalem, I was told, and Herod's men were searching for him. But his followers listened even when they did not understand what their rabbi was talking about. They repeated what he said in their own words, as they heard it, sometimes true to what he said, sometimes not. Then the words were repeated by others until they did not resemble in any way what Jeschu had said.

Jeschu told them of a new way to live and have peace in their lives. Most of them, I knew, would run from him and go back to worship their idols and indulge in their other ways of life. But Jeschu hoped that they would never return to the brutality they once practiced, that they would no longer beat their wives or treat their animals with cruelty. I do not believe that Jeschu thought these people would be transmuted into gods themselves, as he told them they could be.

Another small band of men joined Jeschu and never left him. They prayed and studied his teachings. Jeschu's words seem so simple that I believed anyone willing to listen with an open heart could follow them.

Sometimes Mary walked the miles between towns with Jeschu when he went on his walks in Galilee or to the sea to Caesarea, Samaria, and surrounding places. They took with them a few serious followers. Those who lived with us we called brothers and sisters. These people shared our house and our food and provided Jeschu with any help he needed.

Jeschu liked to go into the garden, pick the fruit, cultivate the plants, and just sit with the plants and the trees as if he, too, were growing there. Mary spent hours with him. Matthias and Sela came often, bringing their child with them. We had other children around: one called Naomi, a beautiful young girl with black, black hair and blue eyes. Naomi's shyness brought her close to my heart. She never tired of working in the preparation of food, cleanup, or any task we needed to have done, and always appeared with a light in her eyes and her heart.

Jeschu's band of followers stayed close to him. I remember their names only vaguely, for they were foreign to me, except for Matthias. One was called Simon and one was called Peter. These men came to the house almost daily. They brought us fish from catches they made in the sea. They seemed to be broad of build, warm and alive, not as crude as the others, and very gentle with Jeschu. They called him Master. I did not like to hear Jeschu called that. He was "Rabbi." The word *rabbi* has respect and honor that the word *master* does not carry. But these people did not understand. Many of them thought of Jeschu as a priest, a prophet, and something of a god. They paid no attention to his human self.

It seemed very long ago, the days when Jeschu was a child, when we wondered what would happen to him, when we fled from Jerusalem, when we went to Egypt, when Jeschu left Egypt. Even his return to us here in Bethlehem seemed long ago. The weeks that passed now passed as minutes. Time seemed to be compressed like a thing that was breathing heavily and must carry a great amount of energy in and out, in and out, so that all might be accomplished in the time set for it.

Our household routine was transformed. There was a milling group of strangers who walked in and out and brought kegs of wine, who set tables and cleansed the utensils, who were forever bringing in water from the well, who were always working in the garden and using our house as a center of activities. When Jeschu was gone, his followers stayed and waited for him. What could happen to Jeschu when he closed the door and left this house still put fright into my heart. Would he be attacked again when he was alone? I did not feel afraid as long as he was surrounded by the people, for they came to him in love, and he returned that love. He healed their sick, sat among them, and worked with them on their problems. He became a roving rabbi. I heard that now there were other ones, walking rabbis no longer tied to the synagogue but going into the villages and performing the ceremonies of the Judaic faith: a wedding here, a circumcision there, a bar mitzvah, a celebration of Passover.

Jeschu did not do that. He did not light the candles. He did not make the prayers. This was what threw the people of the Hebrew community into turmoil: that a man calling himself a rabbi ignored the very roots of Judaism. To them this was blasphemy and traitorous. In their eyes Jeschu was a traitor to the Judaic faith. For what was faith if not built on a pillar of ritual and learned and repeated prayer, all the underpinnings that Jeschu shunned? He would bring faith straight into people's hearts, and through their hearts, straight to their Creator.

Jeschu's way was undoubtedly a shortcut to the glory of recognition of one's being, but it was a difficult shortcut for me to follow. I felt that if I were to do this, I would lose all of myself. I would no longer know who I was or what I should be doing. I would become, in effect, nothing. I could not imagine surrendering myself in my heart to my God. I was lost in a world of care. Yet in some other part of myself I knew that Jeschu spoke the truth.

I thanked God that the gold we received so long ago stretched through all these years, because we used it most carefully and in most exceptional circumstances. Some of it still remained hidden in a bag underneath my house in the ground where no one could find it. When we needed money for tax, travel, food, or anything else, we took one piece of gold. Out of it, we managed to supplement our own sustenance, our own supply, and thus lived without discomfort.

We never asked Jeschu what became of the gold that Mary had sewn into his robe in Alexandria, but he no longer had it. He never questioned us as to where our gold came from or if we had any left. I wondered if he was ever aware at all that Mary had sewed it into his robe. He was not conscious of money as a commodity of exchange. He was positive that God fed us all and that food came in plenty to us all.

I discussed this with him, telling him that it was through diligent work that we earned our right to eat and that if God had not given us the brains to learn and hands to work, he would have fed us as he does insects and birds. But we were given heavier tasks, and among them was to earn our right to food. Therefore, we must concern ourselves with cultivating and growing and buying and selling in trade.

Jeschu agreed that there was certainly something in what I said, but he also said that when he spoke of supply being infinite for man, it was because the Creator does not create without completing the circuit. Whatever supply is required for the created form to exist, to grow, to become what he or it is to be, the Creator provides. Jeschu said that God did not create a beginning without a conclusion. Therefore, belief that there is completed supply means that the person can walk his path without fret or fear of the future.

I understood his point, but I had reservations. When the winds blow and the crop fails because of the lack of water and there is drought and hunger in the land, there is a problem. Whether this problem was caused because we did not see the path we were to follow, or we tried to change the path, or whether it was caused by circumstances we needed to learn to control, we still have the problem. I could not see how a small child who was hungry could find a way to feed himself through faith. The child who was hungry could die of hunger. He could not give his bones nourishment through faith. "How do you explain that?" I asked Jeschu.

Jeschu answered me as he would a child. "Grandmother, let us say this is your child, and you knew you were responsible for its food until it was able to get its own. Then it is you who have faith for the child, and you who can find the food for the child. Those who cannot feed their children and permit starvation have not given the child its right, for there is milk in the breast of a mother, there is food in the roots of plants, in the trees, in the grass, and in the ocean. Everywhere one looks there is a supply of good food. Therefore, if a child starves out of ignorance and blindness of the parents, it is a sad fact that the parents have chosen not to give sustenance to their own."

"Jeschu," I said, "that is philosophy for you to speak like a rabbi, but the truth is that when drought comes and there is no bread, there is no food. There is no bread, and the goats die from lack of water when the streams dry up. How do you blame man for this?"

Jeschu was silent for a while, thinking, before saying anything. "Grandmother, the ways of our Creator are immutable

and not foreseeable. A drought is caused by natural phenom-
enon, and droughts come as plenty comes, in a rhythmic se-
quence. If man can foresee it, he can avoid it. There is
drought also in man and fulfillment in man and drought on
the land and fulfillment on the land. Yet at all times there is
deep beneath the earth water to drink, and at all times there
are fish from the sea, and at all times there are plants bearing
food. Even when man is barren of love himself and does not
supply the earth with its own rhythmic needs, he can find
sustenance. He is not meant to live in fear of starvation."

I looked at Jeschu. "You answer me well and what you
say is true, but the fact is, people do not see these responses
or live in harmony with the earth. So they starve and permit
their children to starve."

"So it is," Jeschu said. "So it is. They must begin to understand how they themselves can give of life to the earth and
bring it back to themselves as a servant of life, as they themselves are servants of life. Else they perish, for the earth itself
will perish. It cannot exist without the life it provides on its
surface."

This conversation I remember word for word. But others
I do not. I liked to sit among the women in the warmth of
the twilight and listen to their stories, for they had many adventures to tell of their lives and how they came to be in my
house. The men would be on the other side of the house in
discussions we were not interested in.

One woman, Hannah, a broad-faced Hebrew woman
with large lips and very dark skin, had left her home, her
children, and her husband and walked here to serve Jeschu.
She was very large, with pendulous breasts, and a large stom-

ach and limbs. I wondered why Hannah would leave her sons and her husband. Jeschu had no need of her services although we would not say so to her.

Hannah said, "I wanted to be alive and happy with my husband. We had two children, Zephan, who was fifteen, and Isaiah, who was ten. We all laughed a lot. I liked to cook and make strange dishes out of foods they never had seen. I would find them in the fields. We had a wonderful array of vegetables. We had carrots and beans, all kinds of beans and great big squashes, melons, eggplants, and every kind of fruit."

Samuel, her husband, was very pleased with her. He looked forward to his sons being old enough to help him in his work. He delivered oil from Judaea into the villages. Sometimes he was gone for many weeks.

"In the summer," Hannah said, her brown eyes wide and beautiful in their glow, "Samuel brought us to the Big Sea. We lived there in a tent, content to feed on fishes and spend long days in the sun. They were days of rest but also a time for Samuel to relax from his winter's work." Hannah paused, remembering, but not with sadness.

"I had always lived near the water, and I missed it when Samuel took me into Kartah, a hilly land away from the water. Samuel and I and the boys learned our songs, and we sang and ate and ran and played. We had a wonderful time.

"In due course, though, living inland became difficult," Hannah said. She did not like having no water to swim in or being a stranger among heathens, for the town contained almost no Hebrews. She became a very silent person. "Samuel stopped talking to me. There was nothing to say. I felt sad and dead."

Hannah explained she grew bitter at the emptiness of her life. "I asked Samuel if I could study Hebrew with the boys. They were learning to read very well and could teach me.

"'That is not a woman's work,' he told me. 'You have enough to do with two sons. You do not need to injure your brain studying the letters of the Hebrew alphabet.'

"But Samuel was away for long weeks," Hannah continued. "I felt strongly I would lose my mind if I could not find something to do. I asked Zephan to teach me the Hebrew alphabet. He did not know his father had forbidden it and so he and his brother taught me the letters—*alef, bet, gimel, dalet, he*—I still remember them. Each letter has its own power and meaning. That's what I wanted to learn."

Then she spent hours on the scrolls her sons brought from their own study with the rabbi. As Samuel was never home during the day, the lessons continued but were never talked about.

One day he returned from a trip a day early. He found Hannah sitting with the boys reciting the prayers she had learned. Samuel went off in a rage such as Hannah had never seen before, although she knew he had a strong temper. He picked up a stick and beat her and the boys. He took the scrolls away and threw them into the fire. From that time on, Hannah never spoke. She served her sons and their father in silence for five years but felt dead. The sons aligned themselves with their father against her and began working with him during the day. She was alone in the daytime with her duties, a slave to three men.

The family never returned to the seashore. Hannah thought she had only death to look forward to. Then one day when she was getting water, she heard Jeschu speaking to a group, and she went among his people and listened to him. Again she heard him speak, and again she followed him. As Jeschu moved around in different places, Hannah began to understand that her sadness came from her anger and her imprisonment. She left her house one day after deciding that she would stay with Jeschu and serve him. So she left, coming to our house and living with us as a sister.

It was not long before Hannah learned to laugh and join in our talk. She shared in our discussions about Jeschu and our lives. She never went back home, but she wished she knew what happened to her sons. "I know they are all right," she said, "for their father loves them, and they were growing up to be like him." She no longer felt anger toward them; she had forgiven them for what she felt they did to her, and she asked forgiveness for her own darkness.

The day drew close when we would be leaving Nazareth and going on our journey to Jerusalem. I would have liked to linger at this point, telling stories about the people around us, but my goal is to ease my suffering and gain release through this chronicle, and the time draws near to move on. I can delay it just a bit longer with a few more stories.

One person who came to our house to live with us was Deborah. She was short and heavy-set, with stringy hair about her hunched shoulders. Always silent, she worked harder than a slave, as if it would drive her bad memories away. She looked at Jeschu with great shining eyes, still beautiful in her wrinkled face. She took his garments to the water and scrubbed them herself. She would let no one else touch his clothes. Mary told us she had fallen in love with a shepherd who was killed by wolves in the mountains. Pregnant and alone in the wild, she had been attacked by some roving wanderers. The child grew to be about five years old, and it, too, died. She told her story in slow starts and stops. She said, "I was dying of grief for my child and for my man. I, too, wanted to die. What did I have to live for? Why was I living when every one I loved was taken from me?"

Deborah heard Jeschu as he was giving consolation and messages of love to a crowd of men and women. She listened. "I felt him," she told us as we sat on some chairs outside our house where we could see the stars and the hills and the sign of a moon coming past the horizon. Deborah said, "I began to breathe very hard as if I couldn't catch my breath. Jeschu's sweet voice penetrated my body, healing it of its pain and grief. I knew that I could accept my losses. I felt peaceful and beautiful. So I followed him here and vowed to serve him for the rest of my life."

She came with her knapsack of clothing and followed him home. People like Deborah were loved by everyone, for they did not create any discord but served happily and willingly and brought warmth to the household. Jeschu became very fond of her. He often reached out to her with his arms and held her to him. This was the blessed work that Jeschu did that never will be told by any one else, for no one else could know it.

I, too, loved Deborah. There was no need for us to share gossip, quarrel, or judge each other and decide whether we were friends upon the basis of our actions. There was simply an understanding and sharing. I did not feel this with some of the young people who came to the house. They were careless with themselves and often had bad smells about them, which

I cannot endure. They gave no thought to helping, although they were willing, if told. That was not my idea of serving. They often expected to be waited upon as much as to wait on others. This, too, I found inconsiderate. Jeschu, however, seemed to understand how they felt, and he did not reprimand them. I had never heard him reprimand a person, except when he had seen cruelty to an animal. I witnessed one such event. A man was beating a very old mule that could hardly move. Jeschu became enraged, pulled the stick away from the man, and threw it on the ground. He said not a word, but the man was frightened and stopped his beating.

Sometimes, as the sunset turned to twilight, we sat outside and sang songs or listened silently to the sounds of nature putting herself to bed.

I knew our lives were going to change when Jeschu decided he must go to Jerusalem to talk with the rabbis there. He wanted to convince them that what he preached was not against their laws, but rather it brought to them a new understanding, a new approach, a new way of living. I felt much better about Jeschu when he remained here with us, but he said it was time for him to go on his way.

He took with him five or six young men. There would be no women on this journey. The men planned to go into villages and give talks where they could. It would be a difficult trip, but his disciples created a strong group of men about him. Thus he was fortified by those who gave him love and shared his food and his life.

I knew that he would suffer on this trip, that there would be those who would turn against him and throw stones at him, and those who would not give him bread. I saw his clothes dirty and his feet bleeding, with no one taking care of him. I was already frightened and worried.

If I had been younger, I would have insisted that Mary and I join him. But I was old. I did not have many years left. I could not sustain such a treacherous journey. I did not want Mary to be subjected to the disturbances as well, for to my mind, she was fragile.

So we stayed in Bethlehem with some other women and attended our own stock, garden, and household, waiting for Jeschu to return. We promised ourselves that if Jeschu did not return for the holy days four months hence, for the Passover, we would join him in Jerusalem. He promised to send us messages by some of those who were accompanying him part of the way. We had to be satisfied with this.

Jeschu left, taking the fresh loaves of bread we had baked, baskets of dried and fresh fruit, and packets of nuts, all carried either on the back of a mule or by his traveling companions. I knew he would be staying at the home of those who found his talks revealing and inspiring, but I wanted to be sure there was food for him and the others. I cautioned Matthias to see that Jeschu ate. Jeschu promised me that he would.

Jeschu was aglow the morning he left. His black hair gleamed against his face, flushed with anticipation of the adventure. He never looked more alive. He was confident, he said, that he would be able to persuade the Sadducees, the Pharisees, and the rabbis of his good faith and of his beliefs, so that they would no longer persecute him or resent his work.

"How could they?" I asked him. "How could they resent what you do when all you teach is that man needs to learn to love his brother?"

"It is the law, Grandmother," Jeschu answered. "It is the law. In their eyes I do not observe the law with proper respect."

I had no answer, for I knew Jeschu did obey the essence of the Mosaic laws. They held true in our house as in all houses of the Judaic faith. We said our ritual prayers and lit our tallow candles, and we did not use the vessels of meat for those of milk. I had heard Jeschu say there was no reason for this. He did not accept it, but he did observe these rules when he stayed in our house.

Jeschu said this was an example of misreading of the scriptures. The many readings of the scriptures were confusing and it was time for simplicity and revisal. The eating of meat with the drinking of milk had nothing to do with the growth of the soul and purification of the spirit, he said.

CHAPTER XIII

CONFLICT

I digress for a few moments, seeing myself in my chair as I watched the receding figures of Jeschu, Matthias, and a small group of men I did not know by name. Deep foreboding and pain pierced my heart. I could feel the agony of that time when I watched my beloved Jeschu, so innocent, so beautiful and pure of motive, go down the hill into a place where people had evil in their hearts and cruelty for their appetite.

I knew as they became disappearing shadows in the distance that they would undergo horrendous experiences. Jeschu represented new life, new spirit, new heart for this earth. Who was his enemy? It was not the Pharisees, not the Sadducees, not the Essenes, not the tribunal, not the Romans. It was the shadow of the Spirit of God. It was in the soul of man, and it was his own human evil. That is the enemy of us all. It has been and will be always, for that which is flesh carries within it that which is decadent and reeks, as well as that which is pure and ascends into light. How can the one exist without the other? How, then, could Jeschu break through the destructive death of the flesh without a battle for his life?

Once more, I remembered Judaea, the hot sands of the desert, the blowing winds, the vast empty spaces, the hills of stone and hills of sand, vineyards of grapes in the valleys, its lakes and waters and rivers that stream across it. Galilee, Judaea, Samaria, and Egypt. I put them in my heart.

Mary and I and the rest of our household once more closed our home to journey into Jerusalem, where we planned to stay while Jeschu preached. We had waited a year, and again Passover was only four months away. Word of his miraculous healing, of his powers, had returned to us. We knew he was alive and doing his work, but neither Mary nor I knew about his health or about the Sadducees and the Pharisees. Were they feeling angrier as Jeschu reached into the hearts of his growing following? Was he talking in the temple, or did he still speak in the fields? Did he still wear the white robe of a wandering holy man? We didn't know the answers.

I dreaded leaving my house, for I was old and had some rheumatism in my body. The journey would be a hard one, taking weeks, so we brought household belongings necessary for our comfort: warm coverings and clothes, linen, herbs for brewing teas, an old underrobe of Ezekiel's that I wore to sleep in and comfort myself with. I did not wish to leave these things, for I knew we would be gone for a long time and might never return.

I was provided a donkey. A friend offered me a camel but this was foreign to me and undignified, and I did not accept it. I think it was offered as a joke, but it was tempting to ride a camel. If I were not so old, I might have been willing to do so. Instead, I rode on a donkey that moved fairly rapidly.

Once we were ready, we loaded the mules and took the donkey. I thought back on our first journey with Mary, the baby, Joseph, and Ezekiel, and I wondered about those years. They passed by so fast, and yet they seemed a century gone. Even now I reach out with my hand for Ezekiel. My heart is with him still. I longed for those days when he took me in his arms to comfort me and keep me from feeling the pain of my fears. His love gave me strength to face the strangeness of our lives.

But Ezekiel was gone, and Mary already lived in quiet acceptance as if she had returned to her own angel state. I know of no other way to describe her absolute surrender to our God Jehovah. She was Hebrew. She obediently followed the Ten Commandments. The smoothness of Mary in her perfection and her love did not seem natural to me. But it was accepted by everyone, especially since she was the mother of Jeschu.

The confusion, of course, was caused by this mixture of heathen and Hebrew. If Jeschu spoke only to his own Hebrew people, he might, in defiance of the Pharisees and the Sadducees, have entered their temples. There, in argument, he might have won some place of respect. But he did not do that.

His thoughts kept coming through me. I could feel Jeschu's embrace. I would tear away from it, for I find the divine love in Jeschu overwhelming, but when I think of him as my grandson, I cannot. I cannot. I cannot. I cannot release him. When I put my foot on the path toward Jerusalem, I was choked with the misery of what was to happen, for I surely knew somewhere within myself that Jeschu's work could not go on. A man speaking of truth, love, fraternity, and the sharing of life among all men must be destroyed by those forces of the earth that seek destruction of all that is divine upon it.

We were mostly women traveling. There were seven of us, including Hannah and Deborah, who would not leave Mary or me. And there were some men, three or four, who took us part of the way on the path to Jerusalem and returned to their homes. Then others joined us, so that we were always guarded, for there was worry that we would be attacked in retaliation for the work Jeschu was doing.

These men were armed with sticks and knives and carried a sack of stones, which they would use if necessary to protect us, although that went against the teachings of Jeschu. It was ever so that the teachings of divine love must encounter the cold facts of the world man has made for himself, in which cruelty is so strong.

We did not travel for too long a time. We rested and shared our evenings with the families who joyfully greeted us along the way. We were shunned by most of our own people, but there were other fine families who knew we were coming. They opened their houses to us so that we could bathe, have hot food, and rest well.

Thus we wound our way into Jerusalem. Jeschu was not there to greet us, but this did not surprise us. He was busy with his Father's work—and he could no longer be concerned with the comfort of his family.

CHAPTER XIV

ANNA IN JERUSALEM

Mary, Hannah, Deborah, and I made our way to the caves with the men guarding us. These caves were not the same ones we stayed in before, but were subterranean cellular structures like grottoes, hidden in the hills. Hebrew tribes lived in them not so very long ago. Now, in Jeschu's time, they were used mainly by people who wished to disappear. It was impossible to find anyone in these subterranean tunnels. They went deep into the earth and were easily guarded because they could be closed off with no entrance visible.

"You will be comfortable here," a young man said. He welcomed us, offered us an herbal drink, and suggested we rest until he could locate Jeschu and tell him of our arrival.

Why had Jeschu chosen to place us and many of his people in these hidden caves? I would not have chosen them for myself. We had many friends in Jerusalem. I could have stayed with one of them. But Jeschu told our guides to take us to the caves. We found ours by walking through a long tunnel into total darkness. We lit candles and wound our way through three different corridors to their end, which opened like a bottleneck outward into a curved room set up with benches and a table, and that was all. We had a water pitcher and a place to put our food. Long dining halls were in another section of the caves.

I lay wearily on my bed, wishing I was back in Bethlehem, remembering the sunshine there even in the winter. The cold of the caves penetrated my bones, and I was not very happy to stay in them. A chill filled the air. Deborah brought in wood and made a fire to warm me. Mary was concerned. I never suffered with chills and did not usually complain, but now I could not control my misery.

"Drink this wine, Mother, and you will flush out the cold," my daughter said, handing me a large cup of dark red wine. I sipped it until its warmth made me drowsy, and I dozed off to sleep as the room warmed.

I slept most fitfully, dreaming of Jeschu. He rode a donkey, and someone, a man in royal garments of purple and gold, knocked him off. I screamed, waking Mary. Then I dreamt about Mary. I saw her as I always saw her, as an angel who came to earth in a body. In my dream, she put her arms around me and said, "Mother, we must endure much in the coming weeks, and you must be strong to survive it. Please do not be so frightened. It is written and ordained as I have told you. You will understand what happens if you will trust Jeschu and me. In time, what Jeschu is doing will be the greatest blessing mankind could know."

I did not like the dream. I told Mary about it. She smiled the tender half-smile I loved to see on her face. "Mother, it was not a dream, for I do feel this way. I must have said it to you, and you must have heard me while we were sleeping. So you see, it was no ordinary dream. We must prepare ourselves for the difficulties ahead. Jeschu is undertaking to change the thinking of man, and a price must be paid for it. He has chosen to do this. Would it not be a sin to destroy or forbid such an act?"

"If I could, I would," I responded. I meant it. I would gladly have forbidden his undertaking. I would return to Alexandria with my grandson where he could work as a carpenter or even be an ordinary rabbi.

Mary nodded in agreement. She would wish this for me, for she knew how deeply I felt toward Jeschu.

I continued, "But Jeschu will not pay any attention to me. I do not know what blessings he could give the world, and I do not care. The people will not love Jeschu for what he is doing. They will kill him. I know they will."

Mary nodded her head in agreement. I saw tears come into her eyes. "If it is so, Mother. It is so."

"Mary, for God's sake . . ." As I heard myself saying it, deep sobs racked my body. She held me and she, too, let the tears fall from her eyes. Then she said, "Let us pray to Jehovah for guidance, for we need it to help us through the hours to come, through these weeks." We lit candles and silently prayed over them.

Then Mary prayed as Jeschu told us to pray: "Oh God, help us in our hours of need. Keep us calm. Keep us in your light. For we understand the task before us, and we will do our work as you have set it before us to do. It is your will, and I serve you, and my mother serves you. We pray that our hearts be opened to you and your guidance. Guide us to help release from Jeschu and those about him such pain and suffering as we can by our care and ministration. Show us the way to be of service to thee and to others. Forgive us, for we do repent of any unkind or evil thought either of us has had, and we repent for our yearning to hold Jeschu close to us and keep him for ourselves. Forgive us and help us. Amen."

Afterward, Mary and I walked arm in arm into the general meeting room, where people gathered, reading or talking. We listened to the many conversations going on, made greetings, and greeted those we had not met before. I found these people strange, coming from all parts of the world. A dark, slender man with wide, deep eyes claimed his home was in Persia, another man was from Rome, and an older woman, not inclined to talk, came from Mesopotamia. I cannot say how these people found their way to Jeschu and the caves. They were quiet spoken, clean, and well behaved. They knew of the teachings of Jeschu, sat at his feet, and followed him during the day.

By the time Jeschu walked into our rooms, I hardly recognized him. He seemed strange to me as if the personal part of him had left and his body was occupied by someone else. Nevertheless, when I first saw him, I came close to him and pressed my body next to his. Waves of energy ran through me.

I cried out as I had done years before, "Jeschu, for God's sake, what have you done to yourself?"

He did not respond. He smiled in a faraway fashion and said to me, "It is good that you are here, Grandmother, but I am sorry you will have to live through these coming months. Much has been foretold, and much will happen. I hope you will be brave and not believe that I have suffered."

I did not know exactly what he meant—I did not want to know—but my heavy heart knew. I think I wanted to die at that moment and not face the terror of what was happening in Jerusalem. For already the air was electric with what was going on. I did not relate this to Jeschu but to a general excitement in the city. I did not believe it was all because of Jeschu. The Romans were there in full regalia, and many of them marched through the streets, tromping on the people whenever they decided to. They pushed into a crowded street, knocking down women and men in their way. One soldier unsheathed his sword, waved it over his head, and charged at a group of men. They scattered so quickly he did not catch anyone, but if he had, he probably would have run his sword through the man and walked away laughing.

Something was happening that we did not know about. I learned the Romans were looking for thieves in the city. They announced that all thieves caught would be crucified or beheaded, no matter whether the poor soul had stolen bread or rubies. There had been a protest against the cutting off of heads. The Romans hung up beheaded victims to show the people what would happen to them if they were caught stealing. Large bands of people wandered in the streets, begging. The quiet Hebraic settlement we knew, when we stopped in Jerusalem before, was gone. The city was overrun by foreign people I did not know.

Jeschu returned to sit among us in the evenings. Where he sat, a glow formed around him. Light, such as a candle sheds, surrounded him. The glow on his face was one of true beauty.

People called him rabbi or master. They did not speak when he sat there. The radiance spread until everyone in the room felt the light. Then, one by one they came to him and put their heads upon his lap. He blessed them. This most incredible scene was imprinted forever in my mind. I, too, found my way to Jeschu and put my head in his lap. He blessed me and raised my face to look into his eyes, and he kissed me on the forehead. The tears rolled down my face, but Jeschu's eyes were far away. He did not contact my eyes as he had in other days. I found my way back to where I had been sitting, feeling old and yearning for Jeschu to be the way he was in his childhood, while at the same time aware of the loving feelings he produced. They were so blissful.

My daughter, too, came and placed her head in Jeschu's lap. He did the same with her. He filled her with light and kissed her on the forehead. He whispered to her, but I did not know what he said. After all had come to Jeschu and sat in the silence, he spoke. But he spoke as if he were not Jeschu. He spoke as if he were in a faraway place, as if another part of himself or another spirit or person spoke through him. The power of his voice sent chills down my spine, but I do not remember the words. I do not think I even heard them at the time, for they were of such power that I absorbed them as if they were water and I was a sponge.

Many words have been attributed to Jeschu, some true words and many not true. The soul-filling light Jeschu put in his talks could never have been transferred to a scroll or print, for they were beyond human conception.

I was still not recovered in my bones from the journey. The long trip kept echoing in my head, so I did nothing to help the others. The women spent most of their days preparing meals and cleaning and tending the babies, while the men prepared other rooms for newcomers and accompanied Jeschu on his walks through Jerusalem.

Mary talked with Jeschu. She said it was difficult to do because there were so many people around him all the time. It was not easy to get to him, but when she had done so, she asked him if he had spoken with the rabbis.

Jeschu said yes. He met with a group of them at the temple. He said it was true that he had lost his temper when he saw the people making money out of sacrifices for the temple, and he tore down some of the stalls where bulls and goats were being sold.

He said the rabbis listened most politely and did not disagree with much of what he said. But he did tell them that he was the true Messiah, the spirit of Isaiah and the healer of men, sent by God. They asked him what proof he had. He answered, "God does not give proof. If you had ears, you would hear. If you had eyes, you would see. And if you were not so concerned with the wealth of the congregations, you would agree."

They told him he had blasphemed them and the temple. "We at this moment strip you of your right to be called rabbi. We excommunicate you from our temple. You will henceforth be known to be a fool. We will spread the word in the city that you are a fool, a pretender, and a hypocrite. You shall be laughed at by everyone. For you have taken upon yourself the role of a messiah, and we say to you that you are not such a one as the Messiah. For such a one would not come to us in sandals in such a simple way, riding a donkey. We would be told in advance. We have not been told. You are blaspheming."

Jeschu said they tore his robe from him and pushed him out of the temple as they would a dog. When he went out of the door, the people gathered around and laughed, as did the rabbis. They pronounced him publicly to be false and a fool. The rabbis went back inside the temple. The people taunted Jeschu. His followers formed columns around him, the crowd dispersed, and Jeschu went into the caves. From that time on, he preached in public places. But whenever he did, people came to jeer, mock and belittle him, not to listen to what he said.

Mary told me this quietly as if I ought to understand. But I was a foolish woman. Still to this day, I weep for my grandson that he should submit himself to such torment and humiliation. I no longer doubted that he was the Messiah. I no longer doubted, for the light and love from his body, the beauty of his soul, and the wisdom of his words shone throughout the cave and everywhere he went. Jeschu was flesh of my flesh. I carry within me even now every dagger that pierced him. For words are daggers piercing into his flesh, and the stones are daggers touching his flesh. How long would he endure this?

Even as he spoke and the Hebrews taunted him, others came to him. They were people who felt that the rabbis of the temple had been hypocritical and the religion itself was being destroyed through the greed and arrogance of its rabbis. These Hebrews joined us in the caves. More and more, some not Hebrews, came, until there were hundreds who were blessed by Jeschu. They called him the Messiah. This love coming to Jeschu from those who followed him seemed to create a protective aura around him so none could hurt him. I felt relieved that he had many people with him at all times and did not go alone into the streets, even though his devoted disciples attracted attention to him. I worried about that.

Yet I knew that Jeschu did not wait for people to surround him or follow him. They came of their own accord. If they had not, he would have walked and spoken alone. For his message and his truth had deepened. Upon the walls of the cave were his words: Blessed are the meek, Blessed are those who endure, I am the Light and the Way.

He spoke now as the Messiah, saying that all those who followed him would sit at the right hand of God and share in the bliss of his spirit, which had come into him, filled him, and was the spirit of the Messiah. For there was the human being, Jeschu, and there was the Jeschu who became the Messiah as if flesh had been replaced by the spirit of the Messiah. The body was no longer conscious of itself as a body, but moved into the light of its being. Its being radiated in holiness from another sphere.

The vision of Jeschu as he was then in those cells is still so overwhelming to me that I would dwell upon it and once more remember the bliss flowing from his body that was so fragile, so thin, so exquisite. The splendor of his love beamed through to all people who opened their hearts to him.

CHAPTER XV

TRAVAIL IN JERUSALEM

It was not yet winter when we arrived in Jerusalem. We got there just as the earth began to lose its green look and the trees lost their leaves. The world was not at its most beautiful, but the harvest was in, and the life of people in the city continued to be active. Jerusalem was not very cold, even in winter. I felt I had to get away from the dampness of the caves and find a room in the city, even though I did not want to leave Mary.

Once in a while Mary came to see me and brought news of Jeschu. I also went to the caves and visited with the families there. Jeschu was seldom around. He ate outside and slept wherever he happened to be. I saw little of him and had little to say to him for weeks at a time.

When winter waned and the spring air returned, heavy storms sometimes blew in Jerusalem. As the winds gusted and the trees swayed, I thought of Jeschu fighting these winds, perhaps holding on to a tree in a field.

One day I saw Jeschu in the street with several of his followers. Curious, I kept my distance, walking slowly behind them to see where they were going. I was hidden from Jeschu by the men around him, but I got glimpses of him. He wore his same white robe. He had removed his headscarf and the rain kept dripping from his face. Water had soaked through his clothes. None of this appeared to bother him. I had been concerned that he did not take care of himself, and I saw at once that he had not.

He was arguing with his men. They did not want him to walk into the city. It was too dangerous. I saw them pulling at him to turn back. I agreed in my heart. I knew this city. It was treacherous. People could come upon you from inside a house within a second and put a knife through your heart, with no one ever seeing what happened.

Jeschu insisted on going forward. I followed behind, even though I had a very hard time doing so. The wind blew me sideways, and Jeschu walked too fast. But I managed because he had to stop and turn away from the force of the rain in order to dry his face with his robe. That gave me time to catch up.

There were no other people in the streets. If Jeschu looked back, he would see me, but he did not turn in my direction. He was too absorbed in his discussion. They were heading toward the temple. That meant trouble, I was sure of it. My heart pounded, and I told myself I ought to return to my house and let them alone. What could I do for Jeschu? I could not help him. I was old and bent and not of any use anymore except in the most menial ways.

The thunder, lightning, and strong winds tore at me, but I determined to follow. Jeschu and the men finally got there.

Women were not permitted to go into the main temple, but there was a court I knew about where the women were permitted to gather and listen to the prayers said in the main prayer room. I went into the courtyard, and from that point I could see Jeschu and his friends. There was no one else around. The place seemed deserted. Jeschu fell on his knees and lifted his arms in prayer to God. I did not hear his words. The others also bent their knees and followed Jeschu. It seemed as if they were all in tears, or else the rain was still pouring from their faces.

I did not hear what they said. I was not supposed to be there or to watch what was going on. I knew Jeschu, too, had been excommunicated and was not permitted to enter the temple. In despair, I sank to my knees and said, "Oh, God, what have I done to offend thee and give this pain to my grandson? What have I done to offend thee? If it is my sin, give it to me and remove it from this holy man who is praying to you now."

I could always cry when I looked into Jeschu's face, for it carried the deep scars of his life. What I did not understand was why he felt he had to live this way. I knew he was the Messiah. I knew it, but I did not understand what it meant. Is not the Messiah one who brings joy and gladness and love to his fellow man? Is not the Messiah one who leads the Hebrews into a life more joyful and wonderful than ever before?

I felt Jeschu was a bedraggled, wet, sad person. He carried glory in him. But to look at him you would never know it. What good was it to know the truth or God when such knowledge brought you to this?

The little band marched out of the temple into the world again. Everyone was still very wet, and I hoped they would return to the caves for clean clothing and some hot soup. I saw that they were walking toward the caves, so I returned to the house where I was staying, my heart heavy.

The time of Passover was nearing. The house had to be scrubbed from its ceiling to its floor in preparation. The furniture had to shine. All ordinary utensils were put away and replaced with special ones. These dishes and utensils were prepared especially for the days of the Passover observance. We used salt to clean them, for we believed it was precious and purifying. We took the salt, rubbed it into our spoons, and polished and polished them. Then we prepared our food and served it with the bread that came unleavened to the Hebrews when Moses took them out of Egypt in such haste that the bread didn't rise.

As we celebrated our feast, we joined in our minds the Hebrews in their flight, telling the stories to our children and saying prayers of thankfulness. We invited the prophet Elijah to return as he promised to do. We left a place for him at the table and hoped he would be our guest.

The household I was living in was very busy, but my heart was so heavy I could not join in the activities. I decided I would go to the caves and stay with Mary. It was as if the memory of the scene at the temple would not leave me. I knew there was much gossip and talk about Jeschu. I heard it on the streets. It was talk about the rabbi who was stirring up the people, claiming he was the Messiah, giving messages to the Jews.

I took a bundle of clothing with me and departed for the caves. Mary was not expecting me. I had not seen much of her, for she seemed to be occupied with the people in the caves. I suddenly missed her and wanted to be with her to get some comfort. I could not endure feeling so sad. "Ezekiel, why did you leave when I need you so, my heart?" I wished I were away from Jerusalem and all the dread it contained.

Even after the storm cleared, and the sun came out, and the earth was bright and clean with blossoms on the trees, I saw a heavy black cloud over the city. Nothing could take that cloud away. Nothing.

Mary greeted me with pleasure. She kept her arm around me as we walked through the caves to her room. I stayed there with her because my former room was now occupied. People were milling about everywhere.

"What about the Passover?" I asked. "Are you not preparing for the Passover?"

Mary nodded. There would be a great celebration here. The kitchens were busy. People were coming in from all of Judaea and Galilee. They were bringing food in preparation for the Passover.

"What about Jeschu?" I asked. "Will he be here?"

Hannah tightened her arms about me but said nothing. I was sure she worried, too. I felt that the people in the caves were not acting right. They spent hours in prayer as they always did. They behaved quietly and talked among themselves, but it seemed to me that it was not quite normal.

"What is the matter?" I asked Hannah. "Has something gone wrong?"

Hannah nodded. "Yes, much has gone wrong, but our Master says that is the way it is supposed to be."

"But what?" I wanted to know. "What is happening?"

Hannah paused, and then she said softly, "You know he is followed now by the spies of Pontius Pilate, the Roman governor, who has been told that our Master is plotting to take away his power. He has been told that our Master is a magician who could destroy him with a wave of the hand. He is afraid of the Master."

So that was it. Not only was Jeschu being persecuted by the Hebrews for defying their laws, but Pontius Pilate also wanted him destroyed. Jeschu must never go out alone. He must stop speaking to crowds. Otherwise a mob will be created to destroy him. So that was what I had been feeling.

Now that I understood what was happening, I wondered what I could do to help Jeschu. What would Ezekiel or Joseph have said?

"Oh, my God, I need you, Ezekiel," I cried in pain. "Ezekiel, if you are in heaven, help me. Help me to save our grandson. Help me to bear this pain and find a way to save him."

His followers were fools, I thought. They were all walking into a trap the clever Pharisees had set up. Jeschu will die, the followers will disband, and no one will ever know who did it. The Hebrews will blame Pontius Pilate, and he will blame the Jews, and Jeschu will be the victim of their plots.

He knew it. He had to know it, and he did not leave. He did not stop it. What good would he be to the world if he were dead? In a few months he would be forgotten. His teachings would be forgotten. No one would remember him except for a few faithful people. I would be an empty old woman who would die of her sorrow.

I determined to do what I could. Although I could not persuade Jeschu to stop talking, there was one person I could talk to who could help. That was Pontius Pilate himself.

There would be a problem. He did not speak Aramaic, I was sure. I did not speak his language. I did not even know the name of it. Then I thought there must be someone at the court of Pontius Pilate who told him what a person said. Otherwise, how could he hold court and listen to grievances? True, our complaints were settled by our rabbi, but not those between Judaean and heathen. Those had to go to court, and the rabbis were then consulted by Pontius Pilate. He made the final decision. The rabbis and Pontius Pilate were very close, I knew, because it was a common complaint that justice could not be had in Jerusalem if the rabbis wished otherwise.

One could go to Pontius Pilate, and he would hear the complaint. But I had no complaint. I wanted to explain to him what Jeschu was doing and to ask him not to hurt him.

As I thought of doing it, I also thought, "What a fool you are, Anna; you cannot let things alone. How can you explain Jeschu to Pontius Pilate? How can you tell him that Jeschu is a holy person who is being persecuted by the very rabbis he is so close to?"

I went to our room of prayer, a dark cell where the everlasting light shines, and sat there for so long Mary came looking for me. I never knew I could pray so hard. I had always left the prayers to Ezekiel because he took care of that part of our lives. But now my prayers became fervent. I could only repeat our eternal prayer. I don't know what it means, except it says, "Oh Jehovah, you are one." Who ever said he wasn't? Whoever said he was two? So I don't understand it, but these are the words we were taught to say when we are dying. Abraham must have said them first. And so I repeated the Hebrew words again and again, the words every Israelite has imbedded in his brain: "Shema Yisrael, Adonai Elohenu, Adonai Echad . . ."

I declared my faith in one God. Was his spirit in Jeschu, and is that why people were saying Jeschu was the Son of God? God could not issue a son, could he? Maybe he could.

Maybe he did. How would I know? I did not understand these things. Maybe it was God's right hand, Elijah, who came into that cave and put his spirit in Mary so that Jeschu had Mary's blood and bone and Elijah's holy spirit.

If Jeschu was a holy spirit, then it was possible he would be able to live no matter what any man did to him. His spirit would not die. He would be protected against death. I was worrying needlessly.

I sat for a long time, tears falling, thoughts falling with them. Then I was aware of a lightness and a strong feeling of love welling up inside me as if a voice had said, "Beloved one, do not weep. All is well."

I looked up and there was Jeschu. He had not spoken, but I knew he had come in answer to my prayers.

He came to where I was sitting. I put my arms around him once again, and he cradled me in his lap like a child. My tears became sobs of agony. Jeschu's eyes seemed huge when he tilted my face up to his. I could see the pain in them. I knew then that he would soon be destroyed. I was sure he knew that I knew.

"I've missed you, my own dearest Grandmother," he said. "It is so good to be with you for a few moments. You are my human side, little one. You are all that is beautiful for me on this earth. You will never know how much I treasure your feelings for me."

"Jeschu," I said, "Go back to Nazareth. You are safe there. Or go to Egypt and teach the people there. Don't stay here. You know what will happen to you if you stay here. You know yourself. Why do you stay?"

Jeschu didn't speak for a long time, but then he said, "I must stay. I don't know why I must do so, but I must. I will be returning soon, my own, to a world I remember and know as well as this one. This is something I cannot talk about to you, for I cannot describe it so that you would understand. But trust me that even if I leave this body—and I will—I will not lose myself. I will remain as I am now."

He smiled. "I make you this promise, Grandmother: When your time comes and you leave this world, you will be with me. I will be waiting for you, and you will know what paradise is. You will know and understand all the things you do not understand now."

He kissed me on the cheek and left me there, wrapped in a feeling of bliss with all pain wiped away.

CHAPTER XVI

ANNA PETITIONS HEROD

I asked some of the men close to Jeschu why they did not go to Pontius Pilate to plead for him, for they all knew that Jeschu had been marked by him.

"Jeschu has forbidden it," they said.

I spoke to Mary, "Would you consider going to Pontius Pilate with me, Mary? We could ask for mercy for Jeschu or try to explain his mission, explain that he did not wish to become King of Judaea."

Mary listened and thought about it. She answered, "Jeschu would not want that, Mother. I could not do it." She did not say that I could not, although I waited for her to do so. Of course, I should have realized she would not tell me what I could do. She never had and would not.

I would have to walk into the court myself and make my plea to Pontius Pilate on my own. I shook at the thought. Never in my life had I entered a court or spoken to a Roman. In my eyes they were cruel and unfeeling beasts, never caring about Judaeans. But I had to do it for my grandson, for his sake. I was convinced that if Pontius Pilate gave me a private audience, I could tell him the truth about Jeschu's mission. Then he would not pursue Jeschu anymore, and he could tell the rabbis not to bother him as well.

My urge to talk with Pontius Pilate was so strong I could not sleep. It is written, I thought, as Mary says. I must go to Pontius Pilate. He must learn the truth. When he knows it, Jeschu will be saved.

I took a long walk up and down the streets of Jerusalem and through the paths of the surrounding hills. Where was I to go and what was I to do in order to see Pontius Pilate and explain the mission my grandson was on so that the procurator would understand and not hurt Jeschu?

It seemed I walked for miles in the warmth of the sun. I felt good, enjoying the spring trees and blossoms. I marveled at the beauty of the floating clouds, some dark, some light, moving swiftly across their world, our world, in changing forms as if they were rushing to an appointed destiny.

Was I a cloud going nowhere? Or was I supposed to be risking this? If my mission was to help Jeschu, and I could persuade Pontius Pilate to listen to what I had to say, then I would surely be helping Jeschu and changing his destiny. If that were written, then it would be safe for Jeschu. If it were not written, his grandmother was simply getting in the way of his destiny. My efforts could cause him more trouble than he had already.

I needed guidance. Who could give me good counsel? Men in the caves, devoted to Jeschu, were wise and warm. I could have talked with them. But if I did, they would tell Jeschu of my plans, and then he would forbid me. If I were to see Pontius Pilate, I must do so on my own responsibility.

"Oh, Father, God of all men, Jehovah, let me do what is right and helpful to Jeschu and let me bring no harm to him or to any other person alive," I prayed.

All of my worry about Pontius Pilate dissolved when I finally got to the court and found out that the procurator refused to see me. I was told at his palace to talk to Herod as Herod was Tetrarch of Galilee and ruled over my province.

There is a long process involved in seeing Herod as I was told when I finally walked into his palace. In the first place, he saw Hebrews only on certain days as their problems were always referred to the high priests of the Hebrews. In the second place, when an Israelite insisted on seeing Herod, he would have to abide by what Herod decreed, even if he gave him a death sentence. The Israelite could not appeal to the rabbis, for he had given up his opportunity to plead with them. He would also be charged with interference if he were trying to get a change made in the laws of Israel since that was not permitted except through the Hebrew courts of the high priests.

The real problem I had was not with the rules but with explaining why I wanted to see Herod. No charges had been brought against Jeschu. I wanted to save him from an accusation no one had made.

How could I explain to Herod's servants and law clerks what my mission was? They would say I was wasting Herod's time. I had to think of a clear reason for seeing him. What could that be? I could not think of anything that would not cause trouble for somebody else, or for myself, or more trouble for Jeschu.

I finally decided to say I wanted to see Herod on a point of Hebrew law that forbade me to enter the synagogue before the men assembled there. He might be curious to hear my argument.

I stepped into the palace entry hall. Never had I seen such splendor. Roman flags and flags I did not recognize decorated the walls. The marble floors were similar to what we had in our own synagogues, but the patterns of black and white marble squares gleamed, polished and shining like mirrors. To one side a man sat at a table. On both sides, tall, slender guardsmen, in their helmets, stood lined against the walls, holding long swords at their hips, ready to draw them.

A man sat next to a clerk who beckoned to me. When I spoke in Aramaic, this man told the clerk what I said and then the clerk told the man what to say to me. I said, "I would like to see Herod in a private talk."

The clerk said, "What about, old woman?" He didn't look up at me or acknowledge me, but the man sitting with him spoke softly as if to tell me not to be afraid. I was afraid, of course. I was shaking, but I managed to answer him.

"I want to talk to him about my grandson who is in danger," I said. I forgot all about the story I had contrived.

"Who is your grandson?"

"Jeschu, the rabbi who is a healer and who walks the streets of Jerusalem."

"He is your grandson?"

"Yes," I answered. "My grandson."

"Come back tomorrow and we will tell you if Herod will see you," the man told me kindly. He shook his head in wonder at me, and then I left.

I couldn't go back to the caves to sit and wait. I found my way to the holy temple nearby and sat in the women's section and prayed to Jehovah, the tears coming fast. "Let me help him," I prayed. "Let me save him from his enemies, for he is a pure saint and a holy man, and he does not deserve to be stoned."

No one disturbed me. I sat there until the afternoon sun waned. I tried to recall Jeschu's life and followed him through his experiences in Egypt, his schooling, his ordainment as a rabbi. I stopped there. I could not account for his growth during the ten years he had traveled around unknown countries. When did he become such a simple person, claiming nothing, asking for nothing, yet endowed with a great glowing love of such power it could not be love of a human source? The other part of my mind kept saying, "He is only a man like other men, a man who understands secrets we do not know and who loves God more than we can understand."

God had chosen men for missions before. He chose Abraham and revealed himself to him, but Abraham lived to a very old age. He was not stoned to death but rewarded with sons and a fruitful life. Moses did not have a very good experience, but he lived to be very old. He was not despised by his people. And David, David had been very human, but he was chosen by God to be loved and to lead his people, and God forgave his sins.

Jeschu, I knew, had never sinned. Jeschu had never hurt anyone. He had never even been a child like other children. The boy had been born wise and knowing, and he devoted his life to more learning, more understanding, and more wisdom. Jeschu offered his life to God, serving him with love and devotion in total faith.

Rabbis controlled their people with threats and force when they thought it necessary. Jeschu never cursed a soul.

He never coveted another man's woman. His body, his heart, his mind, and his soul were concentrated in his work, and his work was to awaken his people to what awaited them in their lives when they learned to listen to their hearts and to give credence to the truth as their teacher.

Why had people learned to hate him so? Often he came home to wash away the blood and dirt from a cut he received from a thrown stone. He would never comment on it. In silence he would clean his wounds and behave as if nothing had happened to him. I knew one day one of those stones would hit him in the head and kill him. It would happen unless the rabbis forbade it, unless Herod or Pontius Pilate took Jeschu away from the danger. I would rather see Jeschu imprisoned than in the danger every day brought.

When I returned to the caves, men and women had gathered together in a meeting hall, eating fruit, vegetables, and cheeses. They beckoned me to join them.

"Where have you been, Mother?" Mary asked me. "Jeschu asked about you. He wanted to spend some time with you."

I told her I had spent the day in the hills enjoying the sun and the air, but I did not tell her about my visit to Herod's palace.

The next morning I left again while Mary was in the kitchen helping with the work there. I went straight to Herod's palace and walked into the hall. The man sitting with the clerk beckoned with his hand for me to come to him.

He said that Herod had agreed to talk with me because I was a woman from Galilee. I was to return at three that afternoon to talk. He shook his head at me and said, "It is a wonder that he agreed. I have never heard of him talking to a woman alone, and a Hebrew woman at that. What is your grandson like? Does Herod know him?"

The clerk frowned at us, and the man turned away without waiting for an answer. I left quickly, for I knew I had to plan what I would say to Herod. I wanted to say very clearly what was on my mind. I no longer was able to talk as well as I did when I was young, alert and filled with sureness of what I thought and felt. I was shaky and uncertain. I only knew how afraid I was for Jeschu. I could not think at all. I left and went first to the temple to pray and to give thanks for the help given me. I returned to the caves to refresh myself with fruit and pomegranate juice. Then I returned to the temple, for no one was there. Everybody was busy with the preparations for the Passover. None had time for Jehovah. He would have to wait until the proper time to be worshipped. This is the way I saw it. Jeschu said that the preparations and the excitement of the holiday took precedence over the message it carried, and so weakened the purpose that the true intent of the celebration was forgotten.

I sat in the temple for a long time until the high sun had lowered halfway between dark and noon. Then I got up and left for the palace.

I asked Jehovah to walk with me. I wished someone stronger and wiser than I could have approached Herod because I knew that I was not qualified to plead with a tetrarch. But he was a father and he might understand. I would appeal to him the best way I knew how.

The fierceness of my feeling for Jeschu was different from that of Mary's. She did not question him, knowing he lived in perfect faith. His followers held him in awe, for he had wrought many, many miracles and he spoke fearlessly to more and more people. No, I did not stand in awe of him. I did not feel that he was above sorrow and pain. I knew he felt them both. I knew that he was human like me and he suffered inside himself from the slurs and jibes and stones of sneering men.

A memory of Jeschu as a young boy came to my mind. He had made and carved four beautiful little boxes: one for Mary, one for Joseph, one for me, and one for Ezekiel. They were different yet close enough to be the same, so that no one was hurt or treated in a special way. I treasured mine and would never part with it. Neither would Mary hers. Jeschu could not have been twelve when he made them, when he carved the stars, the moon, and the symbols of eternity on the boxes made of cedar wood. Something in Herod's palace reminded me of these boxes, and the thought of them comforted me because I could feel Jeschu's pure love in them.

I was ready to face Herod. What was my fear when I compared it to the bravery of my grandson? Herod would not harm an old woman. Why would he want to hurt me? But I could be doing harm to Jeschu.

My knees trembled and my mouth was dry. I thought of my house in Bethlehem and longed to be back there, where I was just an old woman with a family. It was too much. I thought of Ezekiel, the heavenly days we shared when we were young. Now I was alone. My husband would not have permitted me to come to the palace and make supplication for Jeschu, but if I had insisted, he would have come with me. I pretended I could feel his strength, his arms around me. Urgency drove me with its whip. I must tell Herod what Jeschu was like. Herod was the only one with the power to save my grandson.

I moved my lips and prayed silently, "Oh, God of our people and God of the heathens, do not permit such a one as this to be destroyed. Help me, I pray it."

As I walked into Herod's palace, I could feel my stomach tightening into a knot, my heart pounding, my knees shaking. Never had I spoken to a Roman king before, and I was to go before Herod, the tetrarch. I was to plead for my grandson.

I am Anna, mother of Mary, grandmother of Jeschu. Take my word that within the hour of waiting to see Herod, I died many times. I was ready to walk away through fear that I was doing the wrong thing. What if I shamed Jeschu? What if he did not want me to do this thing?

I waited in the hall of the palace until a guardsman came to fetch me to Herod. He beckoned me to follow him through long corridors until I no longer knew where I was. We finally came to some heavy doors, and he knocked. The door was opened, and we went through many fine rooms.

We passed displayed statuary, urns, plants, and benches with low tables. One room had a small pool with red fish swimming in it. Some kind of light flashed out of the pool. It may have been the sun playing against the water. Had I not been so engrossed with my task, I would have stopped to marvel at these wonders, but there was no time. I was taken to Herod, and there I stood.

"Bow," the man said. Another man sitting next to Herod said the word in Hebrew.

"We do not bow to anyone but God," I answered him.

"Put your head to the floor," he almost shouted at me. The guard lifted his sword to prod me.

"No," I said. "I cannot. It is against my religion." Herod must have understood, for he waved the guard away. He beckoned me to him. "You are a good woman," he said in Hebrew. "I admire a person who will not knuckle even to a king."

"I cannot," I said directly to him. "It is not that I would be unwilling, but it is against my religion. It would displease Jehovah."

"I understand," Herod said to me. "I speak simple Hebrew. I do not believe we will need this man." He dismissed him, then asked, "You are the mother of the rabbi Jeschu?"

"I am his grandmother."

"Grandmother?"

"Yes."

"Then where is his mother? Why did she not come to plead for him? And tell me why you are pleading for him. What has he done?"

"He has done nothing," I said. Now I realized the tetrarch looked no different than any other man. He was not overbearing, tall, or extra wide, but soft, white, and small of size, with ordinary features. I might have passed him on the path and not noticed him if there were none around to give him attention.

"I came because he is being persecuted when he is teaching his word," I said. "He harms no one. But claims were made against him. They are untrue."

"Who makes them?" Herod asked me softly.

I did not know how to answer. If I said the priests, I would be questioning their right to judge Jeschu. This would give me no end of problems with them and with Herod. If I said the people, that would not be the truth. And if I said the Romans were doing some of it, I could be accused of treason. I said nothing.

After a few moments he said, "If you stay silent, then nothing can be done. If you are afraid to speak, why have you come? Speak up. No one will harm you. Tell me what you know."

"I will tell you the story," I said, "and then you will know the truth."

"Take your time," he told me. He beckoned to a guard and told him to stay outside and permit no one in. Then he turned to me and said, "I have heard many stories of the miracles your grandson has performed. But it is claimed he is a son of the devil who claims he is the son of God and King of the Jews. Now tell me your story so I can decide for myself what to think."

I had not expected this. How to tell him the story of Jeschu? I cannot recall now in any detail what I said. I was too frightened to remember. I do recall parts: a description of how we were told by the three holy men that Jeschu was a messiah. I did not tell him how Jeschu was born. That could not be told. But he heard of Jeschu's life in Egypt and of his studies of the mysteries, of his studies of the stars, and of his travels in the world. I told him what Jeschu taught as best I could.

The trembling of my knees was such that I thought I would faint if I couldn't sit down. Herod must have seen the color fade from my face, for he got up himself and led me to a bench and then sat there beside me. I was grateful. He did a strange thing. He took my hand and held it in his to comfort me as he could feel my trembling right through my fingers. If

I had not known that I was speaking to a king, I would have thought he was a friend.

"You have given me a different story from the one I heard," Herod said as he looked into my face. What did he see? "I would know more about what your grandson teaches." He spoke Hebrew slowly and not too well, yet I understood his every word. I spoke slowly, too, my lips forming the words carefully so that he could understand easily.

"Jeschu teaches only one thing: we must speak the truth if we are to enter the Kingdom of Heaven. He says that each of us carries within ourself a Kingdom of Heaven. He says all of us are children of God. We carry within ourself a spirit of love that comes from God. When we do not hide from our own feelings, we serve our spirit selves. This spirit is God and brings peace to the earth and to all humans. He says we are judged not by what we eat or how we observe the rituals and laws, but by how truthful we are and how best we serve our own God spirit by loving ourself and all humanity."

I could hardly breathe after those words spilled out. I had recited them and said them as a child recites a speech from memory.

Herod did not speak. I could see he was thinking. Herod Antipas still held my hand while we sat together on a red silk-covered bench, the like of which I had never seen. I looked down at my hand and remembered my mother's, which were toil-worn. Mine still held some youth. This moment could not be forgotten. Herod Antipas, this man held the fate of my people at his will. At a word we could be cut down, destroyed. Our culture, our families, everything we possessed, were also possessed by this man.

My mind raced. Had I sealed Jeschu's fate? Would he be condemned for what I said? I had said that Jeschu put truth and obedience to God before obedience to Rome. How did Herod feel about that? I wondered in panic how it would be if I got up and ran away. As always, I thought of Bethlehem and its peace. And then I remembered Jeschu's words and sought my own inner peace. I would serve my own God spirit. I would serve Jehovah. Whatever I had done I had done with love.

I heard people screaming and shouting outside the palace. Such shouting was always going on. Some person caught in a crime was being tormented by the crowds. They gathered to witness and enjoy the cruelty. It could be Jeschu this time. My heart thundered. If they caught and stoned Jeschu, I would die of pain.

Herod took his hand away and turned his attention to the window for a moment. Then he returned to me. "Your grandson says he is the Messiah."

"I have never heard him say so," I answered. "Others claim it. Perhaps he is."

"Perhaps he is," Herod agreed.

"I know nothing of such things," I confessed. "He carries love in him, and his love is greater to him than his life."

Herod looked at me. "You are old, my dear one, and you have suffered. But you are wise, and you have great spirit."

Sadness overwhelmed me. I was not driven by a great spirit but by a determination to protect my grandson.

"I am a grandmother. I love my grandson."

"Your grandson, it is claimed, wants to be King of the Jews, usurp my throne, and overthrow Rome."

I did not know what to say. But if I stayed silent, would he believe the story to be true?

"My grandson has many enemies who tell many stories," I answered. I saw that I was twisting my fingers, one hand pulling at the other, and I made them be still, quiet, folded together in my lap. "There are stories abroad he would not recognize. I have never heard this one."

"Do you stay nearby when he speaks?"

I had to answer truthfully. "I know nothing of his speeches or of his walks with his friends and disciples. I do not know what he is preaching, but I know my grandson. He has been content to be a carpenter. I cannot understand how he would want to be a king."

Herod stood up, taking me with him. "We can talk no longer. I will do what I can for your grandson, but he has powerful enemies, not only among the Romans who would be rid of him, but among his own people who would have him destroyed. He has stirred up the city and the country-side with miracles and his preaching. Tell him to be quiet and to leave the city. Then when he is forgotten, he can return, and I will speak with him."

I reached out and kissed Herod's hand in gratitude. My eyes took notice of him as a man for the first time. He wore a purple robe trimmed with gold, and when he smiled, he showed white teeth, a rare thing to see. His blond wavy hair fell thick around his face, framing pale blue eyes in pale white skin. He did not look like other Romans, and I did not feel the fear I experienced when I saw them, even though I was very afraid of my mission and what would become of it.

A servant escorted me from the palace. Just outside a man's body swung on a huge cross, the wind blowing him in a sideways push left and right. Probably this man was the object of the shouting I had heard outside. I saw the body, but would not look up to recognize a face. A cry of anguish rose up inside of me. Why must such things be? Our people were once a Semitic tribe from the East. That tribe found Yahweh, one God. They had killed and been killed in his name. The Romans made slaves of people or destroyed them for many reasons, as they were doing to my people now. Why wasn't there enough earth for everybody? Why had we learned to hate and kill and imprison each other as if it were the natural way to be?

That scene of the swinging corpse spoiled my thoughts and brought me to tears again. I was acting like an old woman, a mourner, and not myself. I could no longer dismiss such scenes.

I tried to remember all of my conversation with Herod and the beauty of the rooms we passed through in the palace. I recalled a large black vase embossed in gold with dancing figures on its curved surface. I had stored it in my memory so now it could be taken out and looked at. The figures circling the vase were dancing women with flowing hair, wearing wreaths, filmy veils, and nothing else. How beautiful it was. Then, the horse. I had the memory of it imprinted in my brain forever. I looked at it again. Sculptured in the size of a real horse, this black marble beast had reared up on his hind legs, wild terror on his face. He seemed so alive I could feel that terror and feel his pain. These images kept coming back to me while I wondered whether I should tell Jeschu about my visit and if so, how I should approach him.

It was not necessary for me to think about it. Jeschu evidently knew what I had done, for he walked into the room as soon as I arrived. "Grandmother," he said, "how was your visit?"

I looked up at him. "I don't know, Jeschu. I don't know." I didn't even ask how he knew about it. Jeschu might just know by his own inner eye or someone may have seen me going into the palace.

It didn't matter. I was glad he knew, glad he came to see me and asked. That way I didn't have to decide for myself what to do. I was tempted to say that since he knew I was there, he probably knew what took place, but I didn't. Jeschu just stood there.

"He wants you to leave the city," I said. "He says he can't protect you from the people since you question their laws and claim to be the Messiah."

Jeschu smiled. "Grandmother, dear Anna, beloved of God. You shall be with me always. You are a brave woman. More brave than those who follow me day after day. Your heart is great."

My tears came again. "I am a seventy-year-old woman, Jeschu. I cry all the time. Will you leave Jerusalem, Jeschu? Will you go as Herod has asked? He would talk with you when you are no longer the object of hate."

The light in my grandson's eyes darkened in sadness. He said, "It is tempting. It is very tempting, but I am not going to leave. I cannot do it.

"I must remain here. Try to understand. It is not of my choosing, but a task I have been set to do. Try to realize this so that you will have some peace. There is nothing that can halt what I am to do, no human, no king."

"I know you are of God spirit and not of man spirit, but you are human, too. You have flesh, life, and blood of the earth. Does not that have a right to exist and to teach?"

It happened again. That flood of light, an embrace of bliss as if it came from another world. I was surrounded with a love I cannot describe as Jeschu came up close and embraced me.

"Lord," I cried. "Lord you must be." My words shocked me. There is only one God, I had been taught since childhood. None other can be called "Lord," yet I am calling my grandson "Lord."

"No, grandmother. You must not call me that."

I was not aware of how much time had passed because I could not tell day from night until his light lifted, until the bliss and love softened in my heart to a feeling of peace, and once again Jeschu became visible.

His eyes blazed with glory and the power of love. I wanted to kneel before him, to kiss his feet, to let him know I loved him with my life. But he anticipated my thought and shook his head as he pulled me to him. "No, my sweet one. You cannot do this."

"Oh, Jeschu," I cried. "I know you are our Messiah. I know you are so close to Jehovah that you live within him. I know you are of God spirit and not of man spirit. But why will you not leave?"

Jeschu shook his head. "Do you not see that my task comes before my life? Can you not understand that my life has more value than earthly existence? My life is a symbol. I have been taught so that I can understand the task. I am here only to show the way. I must return."

"To where? To where, Jeschu? Is there another place, another world I do not see? Another place we go when we die?"

"The body is a cloak," Jeschu answered. "The essence is pure, invisible to man, and ever expanding its own consciousness. That consciousness expands when man begins to see himself as one with his God self, his spirit, his power.

Then he can shed the cloak of his personality and live without fear or pain, even on earth."

Jeschu," I cried out at these words, "for the sake of mankind, for our belief in God, do not say these words to those who would punish you. For they will say you blaspheme. I will study what you say, and I will remember it always in my heart. I will try to follow you into this light, and I know you will be waiting for us however long it takes for us to get there, but beloved, do not suffer with your life here. Try now to live it with joy. Do not think you must die. Tell your tormentors that you are not the God of Israel, or the King of the Jews, or anything else like that. Tell them you are going to become a real messiah and that you are thinking of going away to rest and study until you can teach the scriptures as it is given."

Jeschu smiled at me and took my hand away from his arm. "Sweet Grandmother, sweet Anna. I shall see you soon again and you will understand far better what I have said and what it means. Until then, you are blessed, thrice blessed, given the soul and heart of a saint and forever beloved of God. Do not forget that." He walked away.

I sat at the table fastening the words into my memory.

I remembered the words, but I did not understand their meaning. Then Jeschu turned around and came back to my lonely room.

He said, "I came to you knowing what you had done and to thank you for the love you have given me all through my life. I thank you now for what you tried to do. I bless you. You will hear many stories about me, and you already know it is written that I shall die soon. Do not grieve, my own. Do not grieve, for nothing can kill spirit. Nothing can destroy life. It merely escapes its shell. The fruit of the experience remains. I shall tell you now what I told you so long ago. I will not leave the earth but remain as one who pierces the heart of man. You may not understand now, but you will some day. I shall come when I am called, and my name shall be known throughout the world. When I am called, I shall answer as a servant of God."

"What of Mary?"

"She knows. She has always known. She will serve on earth with me. You will see. She is not a mother as you are a mother, but the mother of the earth and the mother of all mankind. In her human form you cannot see this, but out of that form she is an angel and servant of Jehovah." I assented. I had always known it.

CHAPTER XVII

UNDERSTANDING AND
TRANSFORMATION

I am Anna, mother of Mary, grandmother of Jeschu. Take these words and listen well for they carry weight with the world.

It was as if the power of his being would melt my flesh. He became far more luminous, far more alive and of spirit than I ever knew him to be. He had blessed me. I knew he had come to say goodbye.

Sadness overwhelmed me. Jerusalem was cast in a dark cloud, a shadow of such depth that it could be night. I was in Mary's room, in the darkness of the caves. How could I know about clouds outside? Yet I felt them as if they were trailing Jeschu.

For a moment I experienced the meaning of Jeschu's life. Now Jeschu had removed his flesh. I could feel the light spread through him, taking away his substance. It is hard to describe such an inner radiance, a glow superseding the flesh and the man.

I did see it. I did behold it. And for a space of time—I cannot measure it—I, too, felt the power of his love. This love did not embrace persons, or places, or time. This love was of spirit, as if there were nothing more to know. Oh, these are poor words to describe those moments after Jeschu left and the power of his being poured through me.

I sat for a long time. The feeling passed. Once again I thought of Jeschu as a human being like me, not like me, but flesh like me. More than ever, I felt the pang of my longing for him, my anguish that anyone so perfect and so beautiful in his soul must suffer pain.

I called to Mary and cried to her. "Mary, I do not understand. I cannot understand. He is your son and I know you know and I know you suffer even more than I do, but help me to understand what I cannot understand."

I told her about my visit to Herod. She shook her head in wonder.

"How brave you are. But you know that Jeschu cannot leave. He must remain."

"Tell me what is written," I begged. "Tell me what is going to happen. Maybe I can be more like you if I know. Tell me why it is going to happen. I have never been able to understand the way you do."

Mary took my hand, looked into my eyes, and rubbed my cheek with the back of her hand. "Mother, you are our rock, our nest. You are my peace on earth. Do not grieve. I will try to tell you what I know and what I see as happening to Jeschu."

She told me this story as I lay on the bed, candlelight flickering on my daughter's beautiful face, reflecting my mother's delicate features and Ezekiel's sweet mouth.

"When Jeschu was a little boy, he came to me and told me he had strange dreams. He could not understand who he was or where he was. He found himself sitting in a place not on earth and receiving teachings on how to live on earth with his body."

I thought again what a beautiful woman my daughter was, as she reflected for a moment before she continued, "Jeschu was a strange child, so quiet and so thoughtful, so full of wisdom and so patient, unlike other children who fought, played, and screamed at each other."

"Yes, I remember," I answered her.

"Mother, Jeschu was born to be a leader of men, to teach them a new way to love, to awaken them. He was born to me, I believe, because I was a simple and unquestioning child. How blessed that he had a father like Joseph and grandparents like you and my father."

Mary paused. She had never talked like this before. The tears dried in my eyes, and I listened, eager to understand what she was saying.

When she was silent, I urged her on, "Tell me more. When did Jeschu learn he was the Messiah? Does he know of his birth?"

Mary nodded. "He wanted to show a new way to learn and live. He knew that he would leave himself open to the most vicious attacks by his own brother in spirit, who is king of all destructive forces on earth. We know him as Lucifer, and we are frightened of him and his work, but Jeschu knew him as his brother. Seeing Lucifer's evil taking control of men, Jeschu became human in order to counteract the influence of Lucifer.

"This he would do by bringing into our world his own divine spirit. Those who found his spirit and chose to live under its power would be given the Kingdom of Life Everlasting, never to be taken from them."

"But, Mary, all Hebrews know that Jehovah created the world, that his spirit dwells in us and makes us one with him."

Mary answered, "But they do not understand what this means." She paused for a moment. "The Essenes understand. But they do not have the understanding that a spirit may be sent by Jehovah to purify the earth."

"No," I agreed. "They do not believe that, and I don't either. I cannot believe it even when I see the Messiah himself and know it in my heart. I still disbelieve."

"Some day, Mother, some day you will know."

My daughter got up and moved about the room. It had been a long time since I had really looked at her. Now I saw that she was no longer a young girl, but a mature woman. Her beauty remained, but there was a weariness in her. "I wish, Mary, I could be like you."

"Mother, Jeschu has told me many times about my task. He has opened my heart and has healed me of my fear. He has shown me the path that must be followed."

"Oh, my God," I said.

"If you would realize that his suffering is small compared to his glory, Mother, you could accept that Jeschu is bringing into the world a love that may take our people thousands of years to understand. It will remain. His pure love is to remain even if the world shatters."

I could not imagine the world ending. I could not imagine Jeschu leaving his spirit on the earth. Those things were beyond me. I did understand that Jeschu's heart was love. Nevertheless, I did not understand why a holy man of God must pay such a price of suffering on earth to give it.

CHAPTER XVIII

JUDGMENT

Jerusalem's hills grew thick with pilgrims. Hebrews trudged long weary miles, from faraway Rome, Babylonia, Assyria, Alexandria, Greece, and all parts of Judaea and Galilee, to celebrate the holy days in the holy city.

They came in caravans for company and for safety, with their tents and their supplies to be set up in open fields. They moved on stony paths up and down hills of Judaea to the holy city. Passover was approaching, a time when every able Hebrew returned to the temple in Jerusalem for thanksgiving to celebrate the deliverance of our people from slavery in Egypt.

The winds blew hard in the streets, pushing the crowds with their heads bent against it, while clouds gathered and broke. The sun came through, and we hoped it would stay. The winds, leaving a hot breath on our people, weakened, then became still. Suddenly, clouds floated overhead again, threatening our world as their dark, filmy, wispy strands joined together and formed a black blanket, blotting away the sun. I felt the foreboding more than ever. My throat closed. I could not breathe. My eyes stared at the activity on the streets, the donkeys pulling loads, carriages of finely dressed men and women forcing their way through, trying to get past this mass of humanity, carts, horses, goats, and camels. The wares interfering with passage, tiny stalls of merchants selling goods, food, and pottery, made the walking space narrow.

Jeschu did not visit us in the caves for this entire week. I heard stories of him. He was here. He was there. He spoke to crowds of people more often and more rapidly than ever before. He always had with him his ten or twelve apostles. They circled about him and protected him from the stones as much as possible. For the stones were thrown wherever he spoke, not by those listening, but by people placed in far-off places hidden and concealed in higher hills. The shots, thrown or aimed with a sling, came raining down, and some of them hit Jeschu. Others hit his people. Jeschu ignored them, but he often came to the caves bleeding, and we would clean his wounds.

I did not know what took place except what was told me. Hannah went with Jeschu when she could find him. She returned weeping. I asked her, "Why do you weep, woman?" And she answered, "I cannot say. I do not know. But I weep out of my heart, for I cannot contain the pain."

Mary only went with Jeschu once in a while. Then she followed him and stayed apart in the outskirts of the crowd, her face hidden by the headscarf she wound about her face.

The crowds grew. Jeschu's gift of healing was considered miraculous. The lame, the blind, the diseased from everywhere formed lines, begging for the touch of my grandson's hand.

Some kissed his feet and proclaimed him the Messiah. Others shouted, "Here is the King of the Jews." It was a dangerous thing to proclaim where Romans might hear, for it meant death to the one who shouted such words. Those around him hushed the crowd and said, "Do not say this. Do not call him this. For it is not true. His kingdom is within his heart, as is yours."

This is what I could not talk about. I knew such words would be considered blasphemy by the high priests. The high priests did not speak as humans but as judges. Their judgment was not just but reflected the will of those high in position. They did not listen to the supplicant who asked for mercy or who wanted counsel.

No. These judges were often cruel. From the women's court where I have watched, I have heard them condemn a man to death by stoning. What kind of judge is this? Must a man be put to death with stones for a crime so small as stealing a loaf of bread or taking a few shekels from the temple to buy food for his family?

Excommunication was common for those who did not obey the high priests' interpretation of the law. Prosperous men serving as high priests formed the Sanhedrin. They lived as kings themselves, with power in Rome and power over us. The people were angry because they had no voice as they were angry at Rome, angry at the injustices and cruelty that pervaded Jerusalem. But none dared speak, as I dared not speak, for to speak was to be judged and to be judged was to be put to death. It was the way of the world, a world in which Jeschu brought understanding and wisdom. It was sad that one so rare as he must also pay with his life. I knew the judgment of the high priests would be death.

Jeschu defied their Mosaic laws. He denied the interpretation of the laws of Judaea. He challenged the power of the high priests to make judgments as coming from God when they were the words of rabbis. In doing so, he caused himself to be condemned, not only by the high priests, but also by those who trusted the high priests, our very own people.

When I saw Jeschu in the caves, I asked him, "Is it true, Jeschu, that you must go before the high priests? Why do you not do as Herod says and leave Jerusalem until it is over?"

Most patiently did he say again, "Grandmother, I must do as it is written. I cannot change the path of my life. I would if I could, but I cannot. Yes, I go before the high priests, and I will make my statement there. I have been excommunicated, and now I will be condemned to die." His beautiful eyes showed no sign of fear or questioning. He was willing to accept what I could not.

My tears overwhelmed me, and I walked away, unable to bear the scene that came in front of my eyes, that one so pure, so benign, and so loving would be condemned to death by men who could not touch him in holiness. But so it was to be.

Mary and I rested for a long time before we left our cave to stay at the home of Jeschu's friend, Lazarus, in Bethany, where the disciples and followers gathered.

Jeschu had left Bethany by the time we arrived. We were told he had spent the night with his disciples there in the garden. I liked some of them—Peter and John, and also Matthias, not exactly a disciple but a devoted friend of Jeschu. In truth, I did not want Jeschu to be with them. I did not know them, but I felt that they encouraged Jeschu to perform his healing miracles and to speak before the enormous crowds he drew in Jerusalem.

Mary was almost unable to move from the deep pain she felt at seeing her beloved son move toward his death as it was written and told to her so many years ago.

Later, after dawn broke, John came to Mary and said, "I have been with Jeschu. He wants me to stay by your side this day."

Mary, her lips trembling, turned to me. "Mother, I must go with John to be close to my son, but you must remain here in Bethany."

"Let me be with you," I answered. "My grief will be no less staying here, and I will have the comfort of being with you."

We spoke no more but left Bethany in the early spring morning. Rays of the sun broke through and rimmed the early dawn in bright orange and red as if to assure us: "Arise. All is well."

"No. No. Let the sun weep. Let the world darken." I muffled my cry, "This day is a day of mourning so long as this world exists. I decree it." I could not contain myself. The agony in my heart deepened as we neared Jerusalem. My strength left me, and I felt close to fainting. Then my body strengthened as if Ezekiel's arms embraced me. I felt him with me as he held me, as he always had when he thought I was in fear and pain. I felt his strength and comfort pour through me. He restored my heart and for all that day while we listened and watched, I sensed that Ezekiel was beside me, protecting me as much as was possible with his love and healing presence.

John left us in the women's court of the temple to learn where Jeschu was. The court held many women, some who knew Jeschu and others who came out of curiosity. We sat on the floor, our robes concealing our bodies and our heads wrapped in a masking cloth so that we could not be recognized or held to be responsible for the proceedings we were listening to.

Mary whispered, "Mother, are you sure you want to be here?"

I remembered the time of Jeschu's excommunication, when the high priests banished him from the temple as I watched.

I nodded yes. "I am going to be all right," I assured her.

Mary said, "Then I will help you, and you will come with me. But if there is any further procedure, you cannot witness it because I feel it will destroy you."

Mary's eyes, so like Jeschu's, shined with grief and sorrow, but she did not bend in her way of acceptance. She did not cry; she did not bewail the suffering of her son. She did not ask Herod to help him as I had done. Her answer was complete surrender to the will of Yahweh, while I could not in any way believe it was meant to be: that my grandson was undergoing sacrifice of his life to satisfy the commandment of Yahweh. It did not make sense to me. Mary and I held hands and stayed close together.

Jeschu walked before the high priests, led by an elderly man and leader of the Sanhedrin. One high priest asked Jeschu, "Rabbi, it is known that you flout and defy the laws of Moses. Do you deny this?"

Jeschu did not answer.

The high priest said, "Answer."

"Everything you say, I am. I do not deny the laws of Moses or of Jehovah. Rather, I question the laws of man, who has determined the laws in his own eyes and has not heard the meaning of the laws of Jehovah."

Then a high priest said, "And you, you who are a wandering rabbi, do you claim to understand better than the high priests the meaning for those laws?"

Jeschu answered, "I come out of the spirit of the Father and in me dwells his heart and I speak with that heart. Judge it as you will. Is my heart of God?"

The high priests became silent, for the aura of Jeschu's power spread through him across the room and even into the room where we sat. A light so brilliant shined with it that the people gasped.

The women around me said, "He is of God. He is God." I could see the faces of the high priests go white.

One said, "You have power, yes. But it is the power of magic and of the devil, not of God. We condemn you, and the people condemn you. For none shall say the law is not the truth and none shall break the law of Moses. It is blasphemy."

Jeschu answered, "So be it."

A murmur of protest broke out from the men watching. They were awestruck by the power emanating from Jeschu's body. Man murmured to man, frightened and bewildered at this pronouncement on Jeschu. They were not permitted to speak or protest, but among themselves they muttered, "Oh, this is not just. This is not true. This should not be done. But we are weak. We have no words. We have no way to protest to the priests, and we cannot say anything."

Mary said nothing. I turned to her and said, "Is it so written that they must say such words to Jeschu?"

She answered, "It is so written."

John beckoned to us from the door. We got up and followed him outside the temple and waited for Jeschu to appear. When he did, a large crowd surrounded him and jeered and cursed him as a blasphemer.

"They are taking him to the High Priest Caiaphas, who will question him," John told us.

We followed the crowd until we reached the home of Caiaphas. Then John left us and entered the court of the palace. We were not permitted inside. When the men came out, John followed Jeschu. First, he came to us to tell us Jeschu must go to Pontius Pilate for sentencing. He whispered for us to go there, to the fortress of Antonia, where the Roman procurator was staying.

My steps slowed down so that Jeschu was already inside the court by the time we arrived. John went inside with him. Soldiers pushed back the crowds that had gathered to watch. We, too, were kept outside the gate. The soldiers took Jeschu to Pontius Pilate. I do not know what occurred there, but he soon came out again. The procurator had decided to send him to Herod for sentencing, since Jeschu came from Galilee and Herod was King of Galilee. But Herod did not agree that he should do the sentencing. He said the blasphemy and crime had been committed in Jerusalem and therefore was in the jurisdiction of Pontius Pilate. I do not know details of these times as I have never been able to talk about what happened. I know that Herod Antipas returned Jeschu to Pontius Pilate. They had put a scarlet robe on my grandson and a sign saying "King of the Jews."

Jeschu once more returned to Pontius Pilate. I knew there was no hope. We waited outside the gate for what seemed like hours. Mary said to me, "Mother, please go back to the caves, for you must not witness this." Mary's eyes in her pale face showed her pain as clearly as if she had wept as I did.

I longed to do what she said but I could not tear myself away. I had to be a witness. I had to give my grandson what I carried in my heart to help ease his pain. And so I waited with

Mary, Hannah, and a few of those who were close to Jeschu. We formed a small, huddling group. Others I did not recognize came and left, losing interest at the closing of the gates.

The palace doors finally opened. Six soldiers surrounded Jeschu and brought him through the gates. We began our journey of sorrow up Golgotha, following behind at a distance so as not to attract the notice of the soldiers.

When we reached the top, Jeschu said, "I would say farewell to these beloved people, for I go to my Father." He said these words in a loud and ringing voice so that we could hear him and know he was not grieving. The soldiers said, "Very well, King." Then they laughed, all of them, as if they had never heard anything so funny.

One warned, "Do not try to escape or we will kill you."

"I will not try to escape," Jeschu said. He turned around to face us. His voice remained soft and his eyes were luminous and alive. Even through my despair and sorrow, I could feel the reassurance of Jeschu's love pouring out to me.

"Do not grieve, dear ones," Jeschu said. "Do not let your hearts be heavy. For the burden of this injustice lies not with the high priests or with the king but with the evil inherent in the human being that must be destroyed and can be destroyed only through the power man carries within his heart. Such is the power of love. It brings not hate or cruelty or the demands of justice. Rather, it brings truth and wisdom and the understanding that every man is created out of the divine light, the beauty and the manifestation of God's love.

"You will remember many of my words. You may often go hungry to know the meaning of love, so I ask you to remember that within your heart dwells divine wisdom. Go there, then, when you would know the truth, and I will be there with you, for my heart is to be left upon the earth, joined with yours when you call upon me.

"And when you call upon me, call me not by name, but call upon me as the true and real Son of God."

These words were not written down but they were kept in the heads of many. This is how they have stayed with me, but I am sure others may have heard them differently. I know that he asked us not to worship him, but only the God within him.

We stayed upon the mountain, and he prayed with us while the soldiers sat by. They gave him this courtesy out of a belief that he could be righteous in his ways, that he was not a common criminal but a violator of the laws of Judaea, which they did not understand anyway. These men were in command and could permit any privilege they chose.

As more and more Hebrews followed Jeschu, the high priests of the Sanhedrin became alarmed. Could this man with his demonstrations of healing and teachings of love break down the centuries of obedience to the laws of Moses? Destroy their hierarchy? Jeschu never intended to do this. He said, "I am the light and the way. When you call my name, I will answer for I leave my heart in Jerusalem."

Then it was time to nail Jeschu to the cross. I did not know this was to be done. It was the custom, as I have said before, to stone those who must be put to death for violation of the laws. That was the Judaic way and, as cruel as it was, it cannot be compared with the agony of the Roman ways. A stone in the head brings unconsciousness and even a swift death. But a nailing to the cross signifies a painful slow death from heat and thirst and pain. It was the most dreaded of punishments.

A crowd gathered to follow Jeschu up the mount, expressing their remorse and sorrow at such cruel punishment. One said, "Jeschu should be banished into the desert, where he would surely die of thirst and starvation." Another said, "Because he is a rabbi, he should not be put to death like a common criminal." There was much dissension and stirring talk.

The Roman soldiers listened to none of this. Sentence had been passed, and their duty was to carry it out. But they did not add to Jeschu's pain, for he was not a common, ordinary criminal. Very often with common criminals, I was told, the soldiers pierced them with their swords, pricking the condemned man and playing with him until they drove him mad. Such was not the case with Jeschu.

Jeschu's arms stretched across a board. Nails cut into his arms above the wrist. His back was supported below the hips by a tiny board jutting out. His feet, bent at the knee were then nailed to the board. We sat nearby, all of us suffering for the pain Jeschu had to endure. I fainted. Mary knew that I might and was prepared for it. I toppled into her lap and awakened there. I felt the warmth of her body and the soothing stroke of her hand. Jeschu, she told me later, never uttered a sound.

The memory of Jeschu's death still torments me. I can see it clearly: Jeschu nailed to a cross. All wishing to mock him were permitted to do so, for that was also the custom, but none came to berate him. We, as his family, had the right to sit with him. We circled close and said our prayers for the dead and dying. The soldiers stood by staring at us, not feeling our pain or understanding our grief.

We sat there in such piercing agony that I cannot go back to it. I watched my dearly beloved and beautiful grandson gasp for his breath, his head fallen to one side, his nakedness exposed, the thinness of his body revealed. His silence was more painful than if he had cried. Occasionally he looked up and our eyes caught. I could not cry or scream or make a sound of any kind, for it would have caused Jeschu more pain than he was already bearing.

I asked a soldier, "May I give him water?" The soldier said yes and gave me water. I gave it to Jeschu, who spat it out. It was not water. I do not know what it was. It may have been the sour wine the soldiers drank. I do not know. I hope I did not give my grandson vinegar.

The hours went on and on. Jeschu lived. I prayed, "Oh, Jehovah, take him. Do not let him suffer so." All of the light and power of the Messiah, where had it gone? None of it was there with Jeschu. There was only this little lamb, this thin, worn body of my own flesh and blood.

"Where is his holy spirit?" I whispered to Mary. And she answered me, "It has already passed. Only the body is here and suffering. Jeschu has left." I could not see that. I could see the body, and I could see the life still there. Was life not spirit? What was she saying?

As the afternoon wore on, the sun disappeared and black clouds rolled in. I wondered, "Will this day never end? Will night never come? Is it to be forever that Jeschu is to stay in his pain?"

There was a deep moaning from Jeschu and a cry, "Eli. Eli." And then he was gone. His eyes were open, staring. A soldier closed them with coins and drew the nails first from his feet and then his hands. He let the body drop in the dirt.

We covered him with a robe. The men took the body to the caves.

"Watch out for an attack," one of the men told the others. "We may be questioned, or others may claim the body."

The sky turned black with heavy clouds. Lightning flashed across the sky as if in protest of the condemnation visited upon an innocent man. Then thunder blasted, and a downpour of rain drenched our clothes. Here are the tears of heaven for our son, I thought. Some claimed the earth shook. In our suffering, neither Mary nor I noticed. We made a funeral procession ourselves: Mary, Hannah, and I, with those who gathered during the evening, stayed the night into the morning and came with us.

Whether soldiers observed us, I do not know. Soldiers and spies were always about. Whether they were given orders to observe our procession, I cannot tell. I do not think so, for it was of no great importance to the Roman King of Judaea that a man had died for his truth. It did not make him a spy against the crown, and he was no longer a threat to anyone. So they thought little of the results of their action and let us go freely.

Two men carried Jeschu's body. They did not seem to be burdened by his light weight, but the journey from Golgotha into the caves seemed endless. My feet would not hold me, and my body sagged, bent almost double, and I felt myself close to death. Hannah and Mary, their arms about my waist, held me up. They loaned me their strength so that I might make my way with them.

Mary brought me to her room and told me to rest. Mary said a room in the deepest part of the cave had been prepared for Jeschu, where he lay with candles about him, the lights glowing, while all who had been his followers came to him and prayed for him and with him.

I fell asleep from exhaustion in spite of my sorrow. It was as if I would never again draw a breath of happiness. My heart had left with Jeschu, and to this day it has not been replaced.

Not only had I lost my grandson, but I had lost the object of my total devotion, the one to whom I had surrendered my whole life. I did not follow Jeschu as God. I did not see him as a savior, but I gave my heart totally into his own. When his heart was taken from his body, mine went with him. The void opened deep within my soul.

My heart, being a human heart, did not suffer in a way that could be compared to Mary's heart, which had an understanding and knowledge of love far beyond my own. Mary was capable of resigning any experience to the will of her own God. This was how I saw it. Yet I feel the pain now as I did then.

When I awakened, I was told that Jeschu's body had been removed into a crypt deep in the cave and covered with stones where none could touch him. He was to be known as a messiah, a miracle of revelation, Mary said. Therefore, his body was to be kept separate from those who were laid in the burial places of Jerusalem, and it was to be hidden so that none could remove his body or take it away.

I was heartbroken that I had not myself spent some time with Jeschu before his body was carried off. But Mary insisted that I need not see the body, that Jeschu was with me in his spirit, and that I could see him in my mind's eye whenever I asked. Again my crying began, and Mary was hard put to keep tears out of her own eyes. There were none in those days who did not have red eyes and a sorrowing face. It would be a long, long time before the death of Jeschu would dim sufficiently for us to resume our lives.

How can I describe the days following the burial? The daily life in the caves was very quiet. Many people left for their homes in Galilee. Jeschu's disciples also seemed to disappear. Only a few people remained in the caves. Hannah stayed. Others who lived there seemed to be waiting for Jeschu to make a visual appearance. I know it is said that he did—that he appeared to certain persons he knew who had been his followers. They claimed he had risen, and, indeed, I had a vision of him myself standing near my bed, radiant in light, but I put that to my imagination. I do not know whether he came to earth in fact, for many who followed him were vivid in imagination, and some of them could have easily made themselves believe the Savior had returned to them.

Whether his visual self returned, I do not know. That his grave was desecrated I do know. It was said that the high priests would not rest until they saw the body of Jeschu as it lay in the tomb. And so the stones were removed by two high priests. They came to the cave to see for themselves that the body lay in the tomb. When the rocks were taken away, there was no body, but there was a powerful light shining where the body had been and the robe Jeschu had worn when he was buried.

I was told of this by Mary, who said the priests stared, asking, "But where is the body?" Young John, who was there, said, "It was buried here, I do not know where it has gone."

The high priest said, "Someone has stolen it." John answered, "No. We had sealed it as you could see, for it was only unsealed at your command."

The high priests said, "It must have been sealed more than once." And John answered, "That I cannot say, for as I see it, it remains as it was when it was first sealed."

The high priests demanded they be shown where the body lay, but none knew where it lay. They threatened death to John if he did not tell them where it was. John said, "You may destroy my body, but I cannot tell you, for I do not know." John picked up the robe, folded it very carefully, and kept it.

The high priests left, staring, Mary said, into every room and at everyone in the caves. They left to report their findings to the priest and then make a proclamation that they would reward anyone who could tell them of the tomb where Jeschu lay. None came forward, for no one knew and no one knew where the body went, for it has not been seen again. From this you may draw your own conclusion, for I cannot say as I do not know. I do recall that Jeschu had said to me long ago that he had the power to detach his body. As unbelievable as it seems, I do believe he could, that he could have taken his own body from the tomb.

There seemed to be no point to remain in Jerusalem. I longed to return to Bethlehem. Mary, too, said she would like to return. We decided we would go, taking with us Hannah and all others who wished to follow. We would keep our home in Bethlehem, and Mary's house in Nazareth would become a place where those who wished to learn the teachings of Jeschu might come. We would not be disturbed there by the high priests. Bethlehem was a place dedicated to those of the Essene faith, whose teachings were much too close to those of Jeschu for them to interfere. It was not Jeschu's teachings that alienated him from the Essene community but their belief that he had broken the laws of Moses. One day we packed our mules and donkeys and made our way out of Jerusalem.

Jerusalem. Jerusalem. Place of my heart forever. For in it dwells a spirit holy, more holy than the city itself. The city stinks and reeks of its evil, but above it and around it shines the heart of God, never, never to be taken away. I shall never forget you, Jerusalem. I shall never forget the heart that surrounds you to this day. "Oh, let us go back, Mary," I cried. "I cannot leave this city, for my heart is here. Jeschu is here."

My sobs shook my body. Mary took me in her arms. "Oh, Mother, Mother, do not grieve for Jeschu's sake. He is still alive. Do you not see him?"

"No," I sobbed. "I cannot. I cannot leave him. He is here. I know he is still here. I cannot leave this city!"

I turned around and started walking back toward the city. Mary caught me, and Hannah held me while my body shook with my grief, as it is shaking to this hour. I looked back from the hills down on the city. There the sun was shining. I said, "Why is this city not weeping with me? Why does the sun shine upon it? Does it not know? Can it not see? Can it not hear? It is a holy city now, for it bears a light around it that will radiate forever. It is Jeschu's heart, and he gave it to the city. He gave it to this world, and I cannot bear to leave it."

Mary and Hannah kept me moving away from the city, and I finally sat sideways upon a donkey, too weak to walk. Mary and Hannah walked beside me. The tears fell from their eyes as well as from my own. It was a sad caravan that left Jerusalem. None came to say goodbye to us, for all were gone about their business trying to forget the experience of Jeschu's death. It was as if an ocean wave swept over the city and cleansed it of its memory.

CHAPTER XIX

RETURN TO BETHLEHEM

Our party of men and women, perhaps thirty in number, had received permission to leave Jerusalem for Nazareth because we were natives of Galilee under the jurisdiction of Herod. We made our way through the hills and alongside the villages without too much disturbance.

Our comfort came from being together without the need to talk or pretend. In the evenings, when we gathered in the fields along the path to rest, we sang words of Jeschu set to a beat, and then someone gave part of a talk of the words Jeschu had spoken. Some had memorized them as if they were written on the brain itself. Many remembered every word of every talk Jeschu gave in their presence.

Days and evenings passed, and the nights softened with stars flashing in the sky as if they would speak to comfort us. I thought about Jeschu. Was he now at peace and dwelling in the stars? I answered myself, glancing once more back to where the heart of Jerusalem lay. No. Jeschu had remained on earth. His work had just begun. His body was no longer with us. We cannot see him, but Jeschu would not leave the earth until he had fulfilled his task.

When we reached Nazareth, our little weary band sighed with happiness to be in such a familiar place. The village remained peaceful and quiet as we walked in. No one jeered or questioned us. We came to the house Joseph once owned, which now served as a gathering place for Jeschu's followers.

The men who came from Jerusalem with us stayed in the fields under the stars. It was warm and pleasant in the summer air. Mary and I returned to my house in Bethlehem, and we found room for those women who could not sleep outside. The men set about building a shed where they might shelter themselves. Then they sowed the crops. They pruned the fruit trees and vines in both places.

We grew accustomed to sharing our bread and our lives with each other until we became a nucleus of Jeschu's followers in Bethlehem and Nazareth.

Our land flourished. The little place I had built to hide Jeschu remained unseen and hidden, no longer needed, but there forever waiting in case of need.

One among Jeschu's followers, named Peter, recalled Jeschu's teachings. He expounded upon them and taught them as a master might. I see him now as he walked with the grace of God, treading lightly as if lifted from the earth by the very depth of his heart. Still, in measure, he was a man with large girth. Peter carried within him a perfect memory. He said he could recall every tree, every bush, and every building he saw when he traveled with Jeschu. He remembered all of Jeschu's talks and could recall every conversation spoken with him.

Peter dictated the teachings of Jeschu to a young man who wrote them in Aramaic. He put them down faithfully on parchment, which was then wound up tightly and rolled together as if they were the scriptures. Peter said, "I cannot rest until every word that Jeschu spoke has been recorded."

"Well, then," I answered, "You have a lifelong task, for his words came to every one he touched. How can you record all of those?"

Peter smiled. "I did not mean personal conversation, of course, only the talks he gave on the mount, by the sea, to the fishermen, to the people, and the words he spoke as he moved about his mission."

I was very grateful that Jeschu lived in his words and that his words were true. Peter recalled them perfectly, I knew, and Peter understood them. Peter reminded me of a great oak tree whose leaves sheltered the village and whose strength could never die because it drew its sustenance from the very bowels of the earth and lifted its arms into the heavens.

This was Peter. He gave his devotion and love to Jeschu and called him the Messiah. What matters such a name? It could not be worth what it had cost Jeschu. If Jeschu was the anointed one, the Messiah, let it be known because of what he did and not because he had a name. The words Jeschu left, the heart he left, and the very soul of his being that embraced this planet were enough. Through his heart all could know him.

I returned now to Bethlehem where I was not strong enough to participate in the household tasks, the carrying of the water, the spinning, the weaving, the carding, the gathering, and feeding of the animals. All of this was done by others. My only task was to dress in the morning and to walk about, sometimes sitting in the sun, often dreaming of the tender early days before Jeschu was born, of all the prophecies, and of all the change.

So I dreamed by day and slept little by night, for I was tormented by indescribable nightmares. Again and again I saw my grandson on the scaffold, though I did not look up at him nailed there. There he sways, and then I think that this is the way it is with man. He is caught and he swings, he is blind, he is deaf. I wept, and I did not know why I wept so much. Sometimes I called out to Jeschu who died too young, too soon, for no reason I could understand.

I know many have been stoned who were guiltless, many have been excommunicated and abandoned in the desert who were innocent, and many were nailed to the cross without having committed a crime. Although I know others suffered, I have no comfort, no words for myself or others who must bear the pain of losing their beloved innocent children to the cruelty and inhumanity of other human beings.

I cannot believe that humanity is inherently cruel. But from what I saw, there are many walking the earth who are little more than bestial. I cannot talk more of this, for again I wondered if Lucifer has lost to Jeschu. Or if I am mad, Jeschu was mad, Mary was mad, and all of us were mad.

My mind keeps wandering. Surely I do not think so. I do not believe any of us was mad, but rather that our hearts had been pierced with a love not yet recognized or known upon the earth. I cannot tell you what it is. Rather, it must be felt. It has within it a cleansing and a peace, in spite of the sadness.

A peace shone through Mary, who knew the love and the light of Jeschu. Hannah, too, had eyes that shone with light, a swing in her step, and a joy about her as if she and Mary shared an understanding that I did not.

Peter changed after Jeschu's death. "Peter," I said to him, "Why are you so active, so sure that Jeschu is the Messiah? Has he spoken to you? Have you seen him? Do you know where he is?"

Peter looked down at me. He could pick me up with one hand. "Dear Grandmother. Yes, I have seen Jeschu many times. He is here among us, and he moves over the earth."

"I think you are mad," I said to him. "I think we are all mad.

"But, Peter," I added, "I do not know what you speak of. Jeschu would not want you to baptize people in his spirit. His spirit is the Creator's and was not meant to be used by men."

Peter looked at me and was silent. He did not wish to argue, but I became very distraught and said to Mary, "Mary, do you know what Peter wants to do?"

And Mary said, "No. Peter did not tell me."

These are again difficult words for me to say. I have seen much. I have seen Peter pray. I have seen the power come through him to heal a child paralyzed from the hips who then threw away her crutches and walked and cried and hugged Peter.

Peter said, "Thank you, Master." He said Jeschu had come to do the healing and baptize the child. I saw it, and I knew it was so. I knew that Peter had been given the blessings of Jeschu for his work. I did not understand how Jeschu could work his spirit through Peter.

I felt I must leave the earth. My body was too weary, my heart too heavy to live. I could see now as I stood on the brink of departure from life upon the earthly plane that Peter would establish a church, that there would be wars and more crucifixions and more destruction, and there would be hate—and there would be love.

I saw that when she left her body, Mary would become like Jeschu, one who serves humanity on earth through her heart. I wished I might be like Jeschu and Mary and stay and work with them, but I saw during those long days before my spirit returned and my soul passed that I had not yet completed my learning task. I still could not release the belief of my own self as being an all-powerful person who controlled her own destiny through her own will.

I saw that I still did not concede that Jeschu's death was necessary. I did not see him as the spirit of God but only as my grandson who was flesh and blood and who died because of man's destructive nature and his cruelty. My rage and anger, my frustration and fears and doubts had created a barrier that removed me from that part of my own being that waits for me and that is pure and loving and serving. Had I permitted my being to channel itself through me, it would have given me the peace, the wisdom, and the power I so wanted to have. The power within man, Jeschu taught, became the silver chalice shining with so much joy and peace that all who came near it would sip from its contents. But I never understood his words.

As I lay dying by my own choice, people came to me and kissed me farewell with tears. Mary stayed by my side. I said to her, "Mary, I don't want to leave you alone."

Mary smiled. "Mother, I have never been alone from the day Jeschu was born, and even before."

I said, "I know it with my heart, but with my head I worry about you, although I know Hannah and the others will stay with you. They will look after you, will they not?"

Mary smiled, "Yes, Mother, I am well taken care of and very blessed. Do not worry about me as I do not worry about you, for I know you are going to the Father. I know that you are blessed and that you have been blessed in this life. You are a pure and holy woman, even though you do not see it yourself. You have been my strength. You have been my foundation. I want you to know I love you deeply."

When I looked at her, I saw the tears dropping from her eyes. We exchanged a long heartfelt look of farewell.

I dreamt, sleeping and waking. Always Jeschu was approaching, taking my hand and leaving, fading away like a distant star and coming back fully alive and fully aware. Then there would be Mary with me and there would be others caring for me, and then I would sleep and dream of my heart's soul, Ezekiel. And then I felt myself free and alive, no longer embodied in the flesh. Still, I felt the same. I felt my heart and my feelings the same as always: my one and only grandson, my beloved, my light. Why you? Why?